BACKSTAGE

a BOY BAND novel
JACQUELINE E. SMITH

Wind Trail Publishing

Backstage

Wind Trail Publishing
PO Box 830851
Richardson, TX 75083-0851
www.WindTrailPublishing.com

First Paperback Edition, December 2015

ISBN-13: 978-0-9896734-8-8
ISBN-10: 0989673480

Library of Congress Cataloguing-in-Publication Data
Smith, Jacqueline E.
Backstage / Jacqueline E. Smith
Library of Congress Control Number: 2015918868

Cover Design: Wind Trail Publishing

Printed in the United States of America.

I've dedicated enough books to my family and friends. This book is for my cat. And Harry Styles.

CHAPTER 1

"Oh, I've spent my life
Walking on tightropes
Jumping over fences
And crossing bridges
Just to find my way back to you
But now that I'm almost
To the other side
I don't know what to do..."

Song: "Tightropes"
Artist: The Kind of September
From the Album: *Meet Me on the Midway*

If there's one thing I've learned in my almost twenty-one years, it's that life after Happily Ever After is just as complicated and confusing, if not more so, than life before it. I really didn't think it would be, and to be honest, I blame that on Hollywood. All those romance movies would have you believe that once you find that one perfect guy, everything else just magically falls into place.

The real problem with stories like that is that they end before the Ever After part actually begins. The couple finally declares their love for one another and once they kiss, the credits roll. You never see them go back to living their regular lives now that they've made this commitment to one another. Do they go out on lunch dates? Do they take turns folding the laundry or argue over what they need to buy at the grocery store?

Granted, my own Happily Ever After is a little out of the ordinary. For one thing, the only person in the world who knows I'm dating Sam Morneau is his mom, Laurel, and that's because he's never been able to keep a secret from her. For another, we've been best friends practically our entire lives, so it's not like we've had to get used to each other's quirks or eccentricities. And finally, Sam is an internationally acclaimed superstar, which is awesome, but you know, also kind of strange.

Don't get me wrong. I'm used to the idea of Sam being famous. After all, The Kind of September has been one of the most popular bands on the planet for over two years. Their third album, *Meet Me on the Midway*, went platinum within weeks of its release, and I couldn't be more thrilled for them. I don't think any of our friends or families could.

But the fact still stands that my relationship with him will never be normal. And that's fine. I love Sam. I've been in love with him since before I knew what it meant to really be in love. Neither the nature nor normalcy of our relationship matters to me as long as I'm with him. And I think he feels the same way about me. It would be nice if we could actually go out on dates though. *Real* dates. Sure, we can go out for a casual coffee date or hang out as friends at Fisherman's Wharf. But we can't dress up and have dinner at a romantic restaurant or hold hands and watch the sun set out on the pier. Instead, we spend most of our date nights locked up in one of our rooms. Well actually, Laurel never lets us close the door. It doesn't matter that he's twenty years old

2

and one of the most famous people on the planet. Sam will always be her baby boy. It's sweet.

My mom, on the other hand, has no idea that Sam and I are secretly dating. No one in my family does. That's why, when we meet up at my place, my mom has no problem with us closing the door. We've been sneaking up to my room and locking the door since we were twelve years old. Of course, back then, we were swapping Pokémon cards and playing video games on my hand-me-down Play Station, so she really had no reason to be suspicious.

He's actually coming over tonight, but not for a date night. Christmas is only a week away so Sam, Cory, Joni, and I decided to celebrate a little early with a holiday movie night. We would have invited the rest of the guys but Josh and his family are in Hawaii for a tropical Christmas, Oliver and his family are back home in England, and Jesse... well, I just really didn't want to invite Jesse. Joni didn't either, but not for the same reason.

Joni doesn't want Jesse around because he's her ex-boyfriend and even though she swears up and down that she has no problem with him, I think she's still hurt over the fact that he broke up with her. I don't want him around because about three weeks ago, on our very last day in Los Angeles, I walked in on him making out with Cory's supermodel girlfriend, Tara.

Excuse me when I say this but OH MY GOD. Really, Jesse? *Really*? There are hundreds of thousands of single girls all over the world who would date him in a heartbeat, but no. He just had to go for someone else's girlfriend. His best friend's girlfriend. *His ex-girlfriend's twin brother's girlfriend.*

I can't handle this. I really can't.

The worst part wasn't even walking in and catching them. It was the way they reacted to me catching them. I have never been more embarrassed in my life, which is sort of weird considering that I wasn't the one who'd just been caught in an affair which had apparently been going on for

3

three weeks. Three weeks! Cory and Tara haven't even been together for two months and she's already been seeing Jesse behind his back for *three weeks*?

Anyway, once they realized I was standing there, they both started freaking out. Jesse ran and slammed the door shut behind me which, I'm not going to lie to you, startled me a lot more than it should have. Tara began rattling off excuses about how she'd never meant to hurt Cory and how she loved him so much but she loved Jesse too and she just didn't know what to do.

"It's not like I could help it, you know? I mean, I tried, because Cory is such a good guy. But you know how when you feel something for someone? And Jesse couldn't help it, either. There's just that spark. I can't explain it. You won't tell anyone, will you?"

"Uhh..." At that point, I really didn't know what to say. I mean, what do you say in that situation? *Bad Tara! You can't kiss Jesse! You're dating Cory!* But I couldn't even manage that. I was too shocked to form a coherent thought.

I guess Jesse could tell that I was kind of short-circuiting, because he stepped in front of me and placed both hands on my shoulders.

"Melissa," he said in an oddly calm and authoritative voice. "Listen to me. Don't tell anyone about this, okay?"

"I can't - I don't -"

"I know. Just hear me out. Look, we know this is wrong. I hate sneaking around behind Cory's back. But it's like Tara said. We just can't help it. This isn't something that we planned. It just happened. But listen, we're not making any hasty decisions. We're just trying to figure out where this is all going."

"You're trying to figure out where it's *going*?!" I asked, not believing a word that he'd just said. "Jesse, that's what single people say."

"I am single."

"Yeah, but *she's* not!" I pointed at Tara.

"Mel, please, *please* don't tell anyone about this. *Please,* it would ruin everything." Tara was so upset, she sounded like she was about to cry. But to be honest, I didn't feel all that sorry for her. Yeah, it would ruin everything for her. It would ruin her relationship with Cory, her one claim to fame. Although, to be honest, she'd be a lot more famous if she and Jesse got caught. The tabloids would have a field day. Not to mention all the social media fame that would come with it. It's weird, but in the entertainment industry, sometimes scandal is the best thing that can happen to a person.

But apparently, Tara isn't ready for *that* kind of fame yet, since she kept blubbering on and on about how she would do anything I wanted as long as I didn't tell anyone.

Jesse, who was still pretty level-headed, all things considered, went on to list all the other reasons, besides Tara's precious reputation, why I shouldn't tell anyone, the first and foremost of those reasons being the new album. It had only just been released and was doing so well. Any sort of bad press whatsoever might jeopardize the whole group.

I tried arguing back that a secret affair with his bandmate's girlfriend could jeopardize the group also, but he was already on to reminding me about the upcoming world tour and how if word got out about an affair, they'd be letting fans all over the world down and then people might not come to the shows and how it might ruin the tour for Cory and a whole bunch of other nonsense.

Again, I tried to reiterate that this was all very easily avoidable if they just called off the relationship, but I knew the moment I suggested it that it wasn't going to happen. Both Jesse and Tara *really* wanted to keep on seeing each other. And as far as I know, they still are.

I thought that my romance with Sam was the hardest secret I'd ever have to keep. This is so much worse though, because for the first time in my life, I'm keeping a secret from *him*.

5

Okay, so I kept the fact that I've been in love with him for years a secret too, but that's different. He kept the same secret from me.

With this whole Jesse and Tara thing, I feel like I'm lying to him. There have been so many times I've come so close to telling him. A few nights ago, we were lying in my bed in total darkness, his handsome features illuminated only by the moonlight pouring in through my bedroom window. We weren't talking. We weren't kissing. We were just there, together. It was wonderful and intimate and I thought, in that moment, there was nothing in the world that I couldn't or shouldn't tell him. But still, something held me back.

Here's the thing about Sam. He is so loyal to everyone he loves, but he's especially loyal to his bandmates. If I told him, there's no way he would be able to keep that secret from Cory. He'd feel honor-bound to tell him. Unfortunately, it would also be a huge betrayal, not just to Jesse, but to me, because of course, if I had told him, I would have sworn him to secrecy. He already has so much on his plate, I didn't want to burden him with one more thing to fret about. So I didn't tell him. I haven't told anyone. And I haven't talked to either Jesse or Tara since that day. That won't last long, however, since I know Jesse will be at my birthday celebration a few days after Christmas. It's my twenty-first, so Sam has it in his head that we have to have this huge party and invite everyone we know since we'll actually be at home and not holed up in some hotel room in a random city. That's all fine by me, but I really don't know how I'm going to face Jesse. It's going to be so awkward, especially since Cory will be there too. Maybe as long as Tara doesn't show up, though, everything will be fine.

I hope so, anyway.

Right now, I don't want to think about any of that. I want to concentrate on getting my house ready for movie night. Most of the living room area is clean, but the kitchen is a total wreck. I decided to bake Christmas cookies earlier to surprise everyone. I might not be a professional chef, but I make pretty amazing desserts if I do say so myself. I've stocked our refrigerator with milk and fresh eggnog and I also have a whole box of hot cocoa mix waiting in the pantry.

It won't be the party of the year by any means, but it will be very festive. And I think that's what really counts.

CHAPTER 2

"Deep in the dark
You keep on shining
My world is thunder
You're the lightning
I'll stay here alone
Waiting for you
To let go
Of this hold
That you have over me
But I know that
I never will be free
I'm your prisoner..."

Song: "Your Prisoner"
Artist: The Kind of September
From the Album: *17 Times Over*

Sam just texted me to let me know he's heading over a little early. I'm trying not to act as giddy as I feel, but it's difficult. Then again, my entire family knows I have a crush on him, so it's not like they'd think anything was too out of the ordinary. Still, if I act *too* happy about it, they'll know something is up. My thirteen-year-old sister, Brooklyn, especially. Ever since I came home, she's been dropping snarky little comments about my relationship with Sam. My relationship with all the guys, actually.

Last month, this stupid internet rumor broke out that I was dating Oliver. Even though we've both denied it until we're blue in the face, Brooklyn (and quite a few online gossip-mongers), remains unconvinced that there isn't something going on between me and at least one of the guys.

Which okay, fine, there is, but that is not the point.

"So, who's coming to the party tonight again?" she asks me, sitting down on one of our kitchen barstools and watching me put the finishing touches on the last batch of Christmas cookies.

"I told you, it's not a party. Sam, Joni, and Cory are just coming over to watch some movies and hang out."

"In that case, do you think it would be okay if I invited a few of my friends over?"

I glance over the counter at my little sister. She's almost the spitting image of me: light brown eyes, a nose that's a little too long, and a slightly pointed chin. The only difference is her brown hair is naturally curly while mine hangs straight down my back. She's the same Brooklyn I've always known, but something's changed in the past few months I've been away. She looks older. It's a little unsettling.

What's more unsettling, however, is the way she's looking back at me. For the first time, she's not looking at me like her big sister who used to tuck her in at night. She's looking at me the way popular kids in school stare at the dweebs whose notebooks they're planning to flush down the toilet.

Where did she learn that look?

"Which friends?" I ask. A few of her closest friends have met the guys. Some of them have known them almost as long as I have.

"Vivian, Brynn, and Nikki," she replies. I don't recognize those names.

"Who are they?"

"New friends from school."

"Well, do they have to come tonight? I mean, why don't you invite them over tomorrow?" I ask.

"Because I *kind* of told them that Sam would be over at our house tonight and they really, really, *really* want to meet him," Brooklyn confesses. "He won't mind, will he? He loves meeting fans."

"Brooklyn, that's not the problem."

"What is the problem?"

"The problem is he's not working tonight. He's not Sam Morneau tonight. He's just a regular guy who wants to watch movies with his friends without being ambushed."

"My friends won't *ambush* him, Mel. They just want to meet him."

"Well, maybe you can get them backstage passes for Christmas or something."

"Come on, Mel, please? I promise, I'll do whatever you want for the rest of the break."

I sigh. It's really hard to say no to your little sister. But I don't know these girls. I don't know how they'll react when they walk in and see Sam Morneau and Cory Foreman. There might be screaming. There might be crying. There might be fainting. No matter what, I'm fairly certain it will be awkward and stressful for everyone, especially Sam and Cory. This is supposed to be their time to just be themselves. I'm not going to take that away from them.

"I'm sorry, Brooklyn. But I really don't think it's a good idea."

"What if I ask Mom?"

"Mom is going to tell you the exact same thing." I have no idea why Brooklyn would think she would say anything different.

"What about Sam? Will you at least text him and ask him?"

I would do that, but I know Sam and I know that he hates saying no to people even more than I do. I wouldn't go so far as to say he's a people pleaser, but he's definitely a crowd pleaser. He hates disappointing his fans more than just about anything in the world. He'd say yes, not because he wants them to come, but because he doesn't want to tell them not to come.

"No."

"Well then, can *I* text him and ask him?" she pushes.

"Brooklyn, why are you making such a big deal out of this?" By this point, I'm completely exasperated. I have to control my grip, otherwise this tube of red frosting is going to explode in my hand.

"*Because*," she insists. "Vivian, Brynn, and Nikki are three of the coolest girls in school and they were talking about how much they want to see the guys in concert, so I told them that my sister was best friends with them and how they come over all the time and they didn't believe me. So I may have let it slip that Sam was coming over tonight and they *still* didn't believe me. So then I said that they could come over too and I'd prove it to them."

I don't know what to tell her. On the one hand, it makes me sick that these girls are manipulating and provoking my little sister to the point of making her defend herself, and a part of me really wants to invite all of the guys over just to put them in their place. On the other hand, these definitely aren't the kind of girls my sister needs to be hanging around in the first place, nor are they the kind I want anywhere near Sam and Cory.

"Brooklyn, if they're putting you to the test like that, they're not your real friends," I say. "Real friends support each other and believe each other no matter what."

"You don't really remember eighth grade all that well, do you, Mel?"

"And what does that mean?"

"I mean that if you want to survive junior high, you have to be cool."

"You already *are* cool."

"You do realize that you sound like Mom right now," Brooklyn crosses her arms and raises a single eyebrow.

Before I get a chance to respond, she grabs her backpack and stalks out of the room. It's weird to think that she still has a few days of school left before winter break. It seems far too close to Christmas to expect any real commitment to work or classes.

Just then, the doorbell rings, sending my pulse a flutter. I saw him only two days ago for a casual lunch date in Sausalito, but somehow, two days still seems far too long. It's probably because most of the year, I see him every single day. And I'm kind of crazy in love with him.

"I'll get it!" my seven-year-old little brother, Aidan, yells. I can hear his excited footsteps running across the hardwood floor all the way from the kitchen. The door opens. "Sam!"

"Aidan!" Sam exclaims. I can tell by my brother's squeals and shrieks of laughter that Sam has lifted him up off the ground and is probably swinging him around like a carnival ride.

And that's exactly what I see when I arrive in the entry hall a few moments later.

"I think you might be getting a little heavy for this, pal," Sam laughs, hoisting my brother up onto his hip.

"Noooo!" Aidan cries, throwing his head back in anguish.

Sam looks adorable and festive in tight jeans and the tackiest Christmas sweater I've ever seen in my life. It's bright red and it features a light up Christmas tree and enormous, puffy white snowflakes. As always, his dark blond hair is messy and windswept, but his bright and contagious smile lights up his whole face as he sets Aidan back on his feet. That smile broadens when his eyes finally meet mine.

"Hey! Merry Christmas!" he proclaims, picking two large paper bags up off the floor. "I come bearing gifts and Yuletide cheer!"

"Merry Christmas to you, too," I reply as he engulfs me in a warm embrace. I could stay there forever, locked in his arms. Unfortunately, that's not possible, especially with Aidan there, vying for Sam's attention.

"Sam, Sam! Do you want to go play Legos with me?" he asks.

To Aidan, Sam is the big brother he's always wanted. Aidan doesn't care even the tiniest bit that Sam is one of the hottest pop stars on the planet with three multi-platinum albums to his name. All that matters to him is that Sam loves playing Legos and Hot Wheels and has been known, on occasion, to belch the alphabet. Not one of his sexier qualities, I admit, but it does put a huge smile on Aidan's face.

"Do I? I've been waiting all day to play Legos with you!" Sam tells him.

"Alright!" Aidan exclaims and leads Sam into the playroom, where all of his toys are scattered across the floor.

Okay, so watching my boyfriend playing Legos with my little brother is just about the cutest thing ever.

"Would you care to join us?" Sam asks me.

"No! She's boring," Aidan insists.

"Hey!" I rest my hands on my hips and pretend to be cross. Aidan, in response, squints up his eyes and stick out his tongue. "That's alright. I'll just watch you boys while I sit in my corner... All alone..."

"Good," Aidan says.

Sam cracks up.

"Poor Mel. Maybe one day you'll be one of the cool kids."

His remark reminds me of my conversation with Brooklyn. She must know he's here by now, but thankfully, she hasn't come down to pester him about inviting her classmates over. I won't go so far as to call them her friends, because from a big sister standpoint, it sounds like they're bullying her into letting them meet Sam and Cory. And that is not okay with me.

"Speaking of cool kids, that is one stylish sweater," I tell him.

"If you like this, just wait till you see what I brought to change into," he says with a wink.

"Oh, you didn't..." Because of course, I already know what he brought for the actual movie night.

"Oh, I did," he grins.

"I still can't believe it. I can't believe Josh *actually* bought you all matching onesies."

"And it is the most comfortable article of clothing I own. I'm not even joking," Sam says.

He's really not. He loves that thing. We all thought Josh was just kidding when he decided to buy the group matching onesies for Christmas. But nope! You should never, and I mean *never*, underestimate Josh Anthony Cahill. Thankfully, he only bought them for the guys. For Joni and me, he selected a couple of enormous Bath and Body Works gift baskets, which will most certainly come in handy with tour bus season just around the corner. Even with the best hygiene rituals, you still disembark smelling like stale pizza and socks.

"So what else did you bring for tonight?" I ask him.

"Can't tell you. It's a surprise."

Oh God, please don't let it be a onesie.

Once Aidan tires of Legos, he runs up to his room to retrieve the new remote-control helicopter toy that our grandparents bought him as an early Christmas gift. While he's away, Sam stands up, takes my hand, and pulls me into his arms.

"Hello," he smiles down at me.

"Hi," I whisper back.

14

Then, he presses his hand to my cheek, leans down, and kisses me. It's a really good kiss, one I feel all the way down to my toes. After a few moments, he pulls away and smiles down at me.

"Didn't think Aidan would be too interested in seeing that."

"No, probably not," I agree. "Is that what you've got in your bag? A secret stash of mistletoe?"

He just grins and pulls me even closer, so close that I can feel his heart beating in his chest. He brushes his lips across mine, a stray lock of his blond hair tickling my eyelashes. Finally, he looks me in the eye, his blue eyes sparkling with love and mischief.

"Who needs mistletoe?" he murmurs, his voice low and soft.

Then he kisses me again.

CHAPTER 3

"I was promised wonder
An abundance of good things
A life that was carefree
Filled with songs to sing
And I promised myself
I would have it all
By the time I was nineteen
But here I am
Still grasping
At a dream..."

Song: "Carefree"
Artist: The Kind of September
From the Album: *17 Times Over*

Cory and Joni Foreman have been in my life almost as long as Sam has. They moved here when we were in the third grade and our teacher asked me to be Joni's buddy. At first, I was kind of intimidated by her because even back then, she was so smart and assertive, but then she gave me one of her cookies at lunch and that was it. Instant friendship.

When they arrive for our movie night, Cory is already wearing his Christmas onesie from Josh. It's identical to the one that Josh gave the rest of the guys: green with an outlandish pattern of snowflakes and candy canes. All I can say is that Cory and Sam *must* have planned this. Joni, on the other hand, looks cute and comfortable in jeans and a cozy red and white striped sweater that their grandmother knitted for her. I told her to wear pajamas, but even during tour season, Joni isn't really a pajamas-in-public kind of girl. Me on the other hand? I would live in my pajamas if I could.

"Hey, guys!" I greet both of them with a swift hug. "Merry Christmas!"

"You too, Mel!" Cory grins, his brown hair flopping adorably into his big green eyes. The moment he speaks, however, I remember the horrible, awful secret I'm keeping from him, and my insides go cold with shame.

"Where's Sam? Didn't I see his mom's car parked outside?" Joni asks.

"Yeah, you did. He's changing into his movie clothes. Which, you should know, are strikingly similar to yours, Cory," I say.

"What a remarkable coincidence!" Cory feigns innocence.

As if on cue, Sam emerges from the bathroom, his arms and legs looking even longer and lankier than usual in the emerald atrocity that is his Christmas onesie.

"Cory! My brother! That is one spiffy outfit you've got on there!" Sam exclaims.

"Right back atcha, Samuel!"

"Oh God, this is going to be a long night," Joni mutters.

"Admit it Sis, you're just jealous," Cory says.

"Of the fact that you're actually wearing long underwear out in public? No, I'm really not."

"First of all, this is not underwear," Cory corrects her. "Secondly, we're not in public. Are we, Sam?"

"Technically, no. Although -"

17

"Please, I beg you, do *not* give him any ideas!" Joni cuts him off.

"Relax, Jo, we're just kidding," Cory assures her. "Do you think Tara would ever let herself be seen with me again if I went out wearing something like this?"

And there she is. Even though she's not actually here, she still manages to work her way into the conversation and back to the forefront of my mind. I was hoping we might make it at least five minutes without Cory bringing her up, but he's still absolutely smitten with Tara Meeks. Joni texted me just the other day that Cory's constant moping and lovelorn posts on Instagram were about to drive her insane.

"Cory, tonight is supposed to be fun. Please don't ruin it with talk of that toxic harpy." Joni's never really been one to sugarcoat things. Sometimes, I envy her that. I'd love to have the courage to stand up to people and tell them exactly what I'm thinking. But most of the time, I just keep my mouth shut.

Miraculously, Cory never lets anything Joni says about his girlfriend, or anything else, affect him. Maybe because he grew up with her and knows what she's like, he's developed a bit of a natural defense to her harsh rhetoric. Or maybe he's just too in love to care what she thinks of Tara.

I really hope it's the first one.

Although I've got admit, I'm right there with her. The less we talk about Tara tonight, the better. For several reasons.

"One day, Joni, you will get along with my girlfriend," Cory says.

"Sure I will. When you get a new one."

"Hey, who's hungry? I made Christmas cookies!" I announce, hoping to diffuse some of the awkward tension in the room. Or maybe there is no awkward tension. Maybe it's just me. Regardless, I'm changing the subject.

"Oh, you are an angel, aren't you?" Sam asks, wrapping a playful arm around my waist.

18

If we were any two other people on the planet, our secret romance would be blown immediately. But thankfully, Joni and Cory have known us long enough to know that our relationship has never been strictly platonic, even when we were just friends. If that makes any sense at all.

Once we've collected the cookies, drinks, and a variety of other treats that my parents have stashed in the house twenty-four seven, we adjourn to the living room, where I've compiled a mountain of pillows, sheets, and blankets for the perfect holiday movie viewing experience.

Before we can begin, however, Sam announces that it's time for presents.

"Wait a minute, we were supposed to bring presents? We've never done presents before," Joni reminds him.

"Never fret, Jo. This is just a little something I put together on the side. Here you go!" Sam looks way too excited as he passes each of us a rather large gift bag. Mine has a fat, jolly snowman on the cover, Joni's has a reindeer, and Cory's, a trio of candy canes.

My mind is reeling with curiosity as I tear into the blue, white, and green tissue paper inside. I had no idea Sam was planning anything like this. I hope he didn't go to too much trouble.

"What the -?" Joni is the first to reach the gifts inside. I glance over to see her holding up a pair of socks. With Sam's face stitched into them. "What is this?"

"Oh, there's more!" Sam promises.

It turns out I get a pair of socks as well, but instead of Sam's face on the socks, I receive the The Kind of September logo. There's also chap stick, pencils, a diary, earrings, and a purse, all bearing images of the guys.

"Oh, man! This is great, brother!" Cory laughs, pulling out a pair of socks with Josh's face on them. "Where did you find all this stuff?"

"The mall! I was shopping with my mom the other day and we came across this store with a bunch of purple sparkles and earrings and it had all of this swag! I couldn't resist!"

"We don't even sell stuff this good at our concerts!" Cory exclaims, examining his new pair of The Kind of September sunglasses before trying them on.

"Merry Christmas!" Sam exclaims, his arms held out wide, celebrating his own self-decided cleverness. "What do you think, Mel?"

"I never knew how empty my life was before I had your face emblazoned on a lanyard," I laugh.

"That's exactly what I thought too!" Sam grins.

"And here I didn't get you anything as well thought out or heartfelt."

"Nonsense. You made cookies. And while, no, they don't have my face on them, I suppose I'll enjoy eating them anyway."

"Thank you. That's so sweet."

"Don't mention it. It's the least I can do," Sam remarks, settling down next to me and slinging an arm around my shoulders. "Now give me cookies."

For the first movie of the night, Joni insists on a timeless classic: *It's a Wonderful Life*. Sam tries to fight her on it, arguing that it's depressing and he'd rather watch a modern day classic, like *Elf* (which, to be honest, probably isn't the classic that he thinks it is, but I still love the movie). But Joni remains steadfast, and if there's anything our years of friendship with her have taught us, it's that you don't disagree with Joni. Because she always wins. And she's kind of scary.

Once the movie begins, Sam grabs a blanket and tosses it over the two of us. Once we're covered, I feel his hand slip deftly into mine. Playfully, he runs his nails across my palm and traces tiny circles into my skin before finally lacing his fingers through mine. All the while, I'm trying to maintain a neutral express and control my erratically beating heart. It drives me crazy when he plays with my hands! The kind of crazy that makes me want to lose control and throw my arms around his neck. He knows it, too. That's probably why he's smirking. Even out of the corner of my eye, I can see the smug grin on his cheeky face.

He is so satisfied with himself right now. It would be annoying if it wasn't so cute.

Halfway through the movie, my mom arrives home after an evening in the city with a few of her friends. She pokes her head into the living room, says hello, and asks if we want anything.

"Can we order a pizza?" Sam asks.

"Sam, how many years have you been coming over to this house?" my mom teases.

"Thank you, Mrs. Parker," he grins.

"Thanks, Mom."

"Thank you, Cynthia." Ever since she turned eighteen, Joni has had no qualms whatsoever addressing parents by their first names. Or any adults for that matter. Okay, technically, I guess we're adults too, but most of the time, it doesn't feel like it. It's kind of weird, especially since I'm going to be twenty-one in just a short week and a half.

Does everyone feel that way or am I the only one? Like, I always kind of thought that adulthood was just something that happened to you. That eventually, you'd stop feeling immature and out of place and you'd just naturally know how to act and what to say in every situation. That still hasn't happened to me yet.

It hasn't happened to Sam yet either. Just the other day, he pointed out a group of high school kids that looked to be "our age" and I was forced to remind him that we'd been out of high school for almost three years and had, in fact, entered the second decade of our lives. I had to buy him a chocolate ice cream cone after that one.

About ten minutes after my mom orders the pizza, the doorbell rings. Sam leaps up immediately, as though this one pizza is the most exciting thing to ever happen to him in his whole life. It's as if he doesn't eat pizza at *least* three or four times every single week.

"Yes! That was fast!" he exclaims.

"Why don't I get the door?" I ask, rising to my feet as well. For one thing, my face is not one that has been stitched into socks and backpacks and t-shirts all around the world. For another, I'm not wearing a footed onesie.

With a dramatic sigh, Sam reaches down, grabs his wallet, and pulls out two twenty-dollar-bills. "Hurry back!" he exclaims, handing me the money. "I might perish if I do not devour the cheesy-pepperoni-mushroomy goodness that is pizza."

With a playful roll of my eyes, I take the money and make my way into the entry hall. I pause momentarily when I notice Brooklyn creeping down the stairs, apparently hoping to sneak a peek at whoever's at the door.

"Hey," I greet her, hoping that she's moved on from our earlier spat. "You want some pizza?"

"What?" she asks.

"Sam ordered a pizza," I explain, reaching for the doorknob. "I know he eats a lot, but there should be enough to go -"

But the words die in my throat when I realize that I'm not looking at a tall, awkward, teenaged guy delivering a pizza. Instead, I find myself face to face with three girls, all of whom are wearing short dresses, boots, and so much eyeliner that they look like they should be modeling for a glamour magazine.

"Does Brooklyn Parker live here?" the tall, gorgeous blonde in the middle asks me. I'm guessing she's the ringleader. Aren't intimidating blonde girls always the ringleader?

"Um... May I help you?" I ask, praying that they're not who I think they are.

22

"Mel, let me," Brooklyn says, squeezing her way past me and into the doorframe. "Hi, Vivian, Nikki, Brynn. Glad you could make it."

"Brooklyn, what is going on here? I thought I told you tonight wasn't a good night," I remind her through gritted teeth.

"Not *now*, Mel," she hisses back at me.

"So, are you going to invite us in or what?" the girl on the right asks. She's a pretty black girl with long straightened hair and glittery eyeshadow.

"Of course! Come on in!" Brooklyn smiles.

"No!" I hold out an arm, stopping them in their tracks. The third girl, a brunette with dark red lipstick, glares up at me with what I think Sam would refer to as *a stank face*.

"Mel!" Brooklyn sounds horrified. Too bad.

"I'm sorry, girls, but tonight really isn't a good night. I'm afraid you'll have to come back some other time," I inform them.

"Why not?" The blonde demands.

"Um... Someone's sick."

"That's not true! They're here. I promise you, they're here. *That's* Sam's car!" Brooklyn points to the brand new Mercedes that actually belongs to Sam's mom, but whatever.

"Looks like a girl car," the brunette remarks. I don't remember which one she is and honestly, I really don't care. I just want them gone.

"It is. It's our aunt's car. She's the one who's sick," I insist.

"Mel, stop it! Come on! Why won't you let them meet them?" Brooklyn demands.

"Because -"

"Mel? Is everything okay?" Sam calls, stepping out of the living room and into the entry hall.

Oh, not good.

The three girls freeze, eyes wide, mouths agape, and for half a second, I genuinely believe that maybe there won't

23

be a meltdown. Maybe they'll handle meeting their favorite pop star with maturity and poise.

"AAAAAAAAAHHHH!"

Or maybe not.

"Oh my GOD, it's really him! It's really you! It's *Sam Morneau*! I love you Sam!" the blonde yells, running over to him. The stank face brunette follows suit, while the girl with the glitter sobs so hard she can barely breathe.

"Will you take a picture with me? Can I post it on my Instagram!?"

"Oh my God, *no one* is going to believe this. We have to take like, a million pictures."

"Will you follow me on Twitter?"

"Can I just *hug* you?"

Now Sam is usually great around fans. When he's expecting to see them, that is. And there are restrictions in place. Like at meet-and-greets. There are body guards and security all around, so the fans are usually on their best behavior. Even when Sam meets fans on the street, they're generally very composed and gracious. *This*, as I predicted earlier, is an ambush.

"*What* is going on in here?" Joni appears with Cory tagging along behind her.

"CORY FOREMAN!" The three girls scream again.

"Cory! You're my favorite!" Glitter Girl manages through her sobs.

"I need a picture with you, too!" Stank Face exclaims.

"Can we get a picture of the three of us with both of you?"

"No! I want the picture of just me and them. I don't want you two in it."

"Oh my God, I'm SHAKING! Like, I'm literally shaking! Look at me!"

"Will you sing something for us? Like, just the two of you?"

"Sam, will you be my first kiss? Please?"

"Cory, I love you so much."

"*Who* are you?!" Joni yells above the girls' constant screaming.

"I'm Vivian! This is Nikki and Brynn," the blonde answers. "We're friends of Brooklyn's from school. Thank you so much for having us over! This is seriously the best night of my life!"

"I can't believe you really know them! Are you still dating Tara Meeks, Cory? Do you think you could send her a picture of me? I'd love to be a model like her someday!"

"Will you PLEASE follow me on Twitter?"

"Can I have your phone number?"

"Oh my GOD, I can't believe we're friends with The Kind of September!"

"Is everything okay down here?" My mom asks, appearing at the foot of the stairs.

"Oh yeah. Everything's fine, Mom. I just invited a few friends from school over," Brooklyn answers above the deafening chatter of her three "friends."

"What?" Mom asks. "Brooklyn, you knew Sam and Cory were going to be here tonight."

"Yeah. *That's* why she invited them over." I'm fully aware that I'm ratting out my little sister but I really don't care. I'm really, truly pissed off right now. Brooklyn has been to the guys' concerts. She knows how some of the fans get. *Why* did she think this was okay?

Meanwhile, poor Sam and Cory are posing for picture after picture in those matching onesies that they're wearing. They're both doing their best to smile and act appreciative, but neither of them was prepared to deal with this tonight. This should have been a fun night to relax and enjoy the holidays! Not this!

"Brooklyn, did you ask Sam and Cory if they were okay with this?" Mom asks.

"I told Mel to ask them if it would be okay, which she clearly *didn't*."

25

"No, I didn't because I didn't want to put Sam and Cory on the spot like that," I explain.

"Brooklyn, you need to ask your friends to leave," Mom says.

"But -"

"No buts. Do it. Or I will." Mom gives Brooklyn the Look. You know, the one that all parents know. The one that rips right through your soul and plagues you with guilt until you feel like the worst person to ever walk the face of the planet? That Look.

"Fine," Brooklyn heaves an incredibly melodramatic sigh. "Thanks a lot, Mel."

"What did I do?" I ask. But Brooklyn doesn't respond. Instead, she sulks over to the three girls and tries her best to usher them back out the door.

"What?! But I thought we were watching a movie!" Glitter Girl shrieks.

"Why can't we stay a little longer?"

"Sam! Sam, I love you!"

"Can you at least get us backstage passes?"

Once Joni and I have finally managed to shove them out the door, a strange sense of calm and relief, like one you might feel after a tornado passes through, settles over the entry hall. Brooklyn gives me one final icy glare before storming up to her room and slamming the door. The rest of us stand in awkward, slightly bewildered silence when the doorbell rings again.

Sam looks over at me.

"Man, I hope that's actually the pizza."

CHAPTER 4

"After all this time
I think I'm gonna let you go
I don't need a reason why
You told me time and time again
That I wasn't the one for you
Now I'm thinking you were right..."

Song: "Not the One"
Artist: The Kind of September
From the Album: *Meet Me on the Midway*

There is a simple truth concerning those of us born on or within a few days of Christmas: When it comes to gifts and birthday celebrations, we get ripped off. Big time.

My birthday is December 28 and for as long as I can remember, friends and family members have always taken the killing-two-birds-with-one-stone approach. All Holiday Babies know what I'm talking about: the infamous Christmas and Birthday Gift Pack Combo.

To be fair, it really doesn't bother me all that much anymore. It used to when I was little. Unlike all my friends who had massive birthday celebrations, mine was always treated more like an afterthought to Christmas than an actual birthday. Everyone is still recovering from all the good food and festivities and onslaught of gifts. No one really has the energy or the money for another celebration just three days later. Even if they did, at least half of the people I know go out of town for the holidays so they're not around for my birthday anyway.

That brings me back to my original point. Being born around Christmastime is kind of a bummer.

This year, however, I'm turning twenty-one and Sam and Joni have both assured me that it's going to be the best birthday ever. Sam's enthusiasm doesn't really surprise me. He gets excited for pretty much everything. But Joni isn't the type to go out of her way to make things special, so the fact that she's so eager to make my birthday the best ever, well, it makes me feel *really* special.

Last week, after the movie night fiasco, Sam stuck around after Cory and Joni left to kiss me goodnight and to tell me, "Think about what you want for your birthday. And don't say something generic like a bracelet or ice skates. I want to get you something really cool. Something really unique that no one else has ever thought to get you."

I almost told him that no one had ever offered to get me ice skates, nor had I ever thought to ask for them since I can't skate, but he was so sweet and sincere that I didn't want to ruin the moment.

"I'll try to think of something," I promised him. "Although, I don't think I'll be able to come up with anything half as good as my The Kind of September socks."

"Oh, well, *nothing* is as good as that," he laughed before kissing me one last time.

Now it's the day before my birthday and I've finally decided what I'm going to ask for. I'll be the first to admit that I'm not very good at presents, giving or receiving. It's not that I don't like presents, it's just that I'm so indecisive I can never figure out what to get for people or what I'd like them to get for me. Gifts, to me, are better when they're spontaneous. But I've given this a lot of thought, and I'm positive it's what I want.

So when Sam arrives a few minutes later to pick me up for a pre-birthday outing to the city, I ask, "So, remember last week when you told me to think about what I wanted for my birthday?"

"I do," he answers with a grin.

"I know what I want."

"It better be good. I'm not taking you to Target."

"I don't want to go to Target," I assure him.

"Good."

"I want to get a tattoo."

And at that, Sam's face lights up.

"Really?" he asks.

Sam is something of a tattoo enthusiast. He got his first, an intricate Tree of Life, on his eighteenth birthday, before we'd even graduated high school. Josh, Jesse, and Oliver followed along in his footsteps shortly thereafter. Cory is the only one who doesn't have a tattoo. He doesn't blatantly disapprove of them or anything. He just has no interest in getting one. Joni, on the other hand, *hates* tattoos. Always has. When the guys first started getting them, she threw an absolute fit.

"Why would you want to mark up your bodies like that?!" she'd demanded. "Tattoos are so tacky! You don't look edgy or sexy. You look like an idiot who paid an even bigger idiot to doodle on your skin. *With a needle.*"

Needless to say, I've never had the guts to tell her that I think tattoos are actually pretty cool. Or that I've always secretly wanted one.

Well, that's not entirely true. I've mentioned once or twice that if I were going to get a tattoo, it would be something small, probably on my wrist or the base of my neck. I guess Joni didn't think I actually meant it though, because she

29

laughed and made an offhanded remark about how she couldn't picture me with a tattoo.

Guess that's about to change!

"Really," I tell Sam.

"Alright! I'm going to call Xander right now. Oh my God, I'm so excited," Sam announces, whipping out his phone. Xander Mendes is his tattoo guy. He owns his own parlor in downtown San Francisco and thanks to his association with Sam, he's in pretty high demand. That also means, however, that Sam can call him up whenever he wants and schedule an appointment. "Hey, Xander! What's up, buddy? Listen, do you have any openings today? No, it's not for me, it's for my girl - my uh, my friend. Yeah, tomorrow's her birthday. The big twenty-one! So, you think you can schedule us in? Great! Thanks, man. I appreciate it." He hangs up the phone and looks at me. "Xander says to come on down!"

Wow. That was fast.

"Great!" I exclaim, hoping that Sam can't tell how nervous I suddenly am. I *do* want the tattoo. I do. But it is a nerve-wracking experience. And it's all happening so quickly!

But hey, Sam will be right there with me. I have nothing to worry about at all.

...

Due to Sam's predisposition to attract adoring crowds and induce fangirl riots, we park in an alley behind Xander's tattoo parlor, Half Moon Ink, and slip in through the back door. Xander is waiting there to greet us.

He looks like your typical tattoo guy: about twenty-five years old, black spiky hair, ear gages, a nose ring, and of course, every inch of skin on his legs, arms, and the back of his neck, is a regular painted canvas of tattoo art, most of which are his own designs.

"Good to see you, buddy. It's been a while," Xander greets Sam. Then he turns to me. "And you must be the birthday girl. Are you a virgin?"

"Excuse me?!" I yelp. Who *asks* something like that?!

"A *tattoo* virgin," Sam explains, very blatantly trying not to laugh out loud.

"I guess that answers that," Xander snickers.

I remind myself that he's Sam's friend and that he does excellent work, but I can't stop the blush creeping up my cheeks. This is not off to a very good start. Sam seems to sense my discomfort.

"Okay, okay, that's enough," he tells Xander. "Yes, this is her first tattoo."

"Awesome. Good for you," Xander grins. "I'm sorry if I made you feel awkward. It's kind of my M.O. around pretty girls."

Aw. That's nice of him to say.

"It's okay. I'm kind of an awkward person myself," I assure him.

"Well, I hear awkward people make awkwardly cute couples," Xander winks.

I'm not sure how to respond to that, but Sam certainly does.

"Yes, well, unfortunately she's off the market," he remarks pointedly. I can't believe it. Is he jealous? How cute is that?

"Just my luck," Xander sighs. "Right then, let's get you back and settled in a room," he announces and leads us down a hall full of vintage rock and roll posters, as well as framed photos of Xander and a number of musicians and other celebrities. I'm sure Sam and the rest of the guys are up there somewhere.

The room itself is decorated in a similar fashion. Also framed on the wall, however, are Xander's credentials and a picture of him and a pit bull puppy. He catches me eyeing it.

31

"That's my baby Sophie. She's not so little anymore though. She'll be two in March."

"She's precious," I tell him.

"You got pets?" he asks.

"No. I love animals though."

"All good people do," Xander grins. "Now, have you given any thought as to what you want?"

"I have," I answer. "I think I'd like a snowflake on the inside of my left wrist."

"I can do that. But can I make a suggestion?"

"Sure."

"Why not a pair of snowflakes? One snowflake looks so lonely, a bit unnatural. A pair of snowflakes will give the piece an asymmetric, more artistic vibe. But of course, this is your body, your tattoo. I'm here to give you what you want."

"Actually, I really like the idea of two snowflakes," I tell him.

"Great! Why don't I draw up a few sketches for you and you can pick which one you like best?"

"Sounds good."

He disappears into an adjacent office, leaving Sam and me alone, standing next to a chair that reminds me of one I'd see at the dentist's. Glancing over at the counter, I see an assortment of colorful inks and silver instruments inside clear plastic packaging. At least I know everything here is sterile.

Sam, meanwhile, wraps a discreet arm around my waist and smiles. "You ready for this?"

"Oh yeah," I reply. And I am. Still a bit jittery. After all, I am about to let a guy etch a permanent drawing into my skin with a needle. But overall, prepared.

"You're gonna do great," he murmurs, kissing my temple.

When Xander returns a few minutes later, he's carrying five different sketches of snowflakes of all different sizes. I choose the one that looks the most elegant: two

32

snowflakes, one large, one small, that look to be dancing through the air as they fall.

"I like that one best too," Sam agrees.

"Alright. Let's do this," Xander announces and slips on a pair of sanitary gloves. While he prepares his tattoo machine, he asks, "Okay, I'm curious. Why the snowflakes? Because you're a winter baby?"

I guess the short, simple answer to that question is yes. However, it's a lot more personal than that. I've always loved the idea of snow, though I hadn't really experienced it very much until recently. The tattoo is also an homage to the guys' song, "Snowlight," which Sam claims I helped to inspire.

Xander probably doesn't need to know all that though.

"Yeah. That and I just like snowflakes," I tell him.

"Fair enough," he says. "Okay, I think we're ready."

Before the needle goes in, he sterilizes the inside of my wrist with a cool, antibacterial wipe. Then, he presses the sketch I chose down onto my skin and removes it quickly, leaving a purple image of the design on my wrist.

"Whoa." I'm probably way more impressed than I should be. "How'd you do that?"

"Did you ever do those temporary stick-on tattoos with water?" he asks. "Same basic idea." And then, just like it's no big deal at all, he picks up the tattoo machine and presses the needle to my skin.

It turns out to be way less nerve-wracking and painful than I anticipated. It feels more like a vibrating pen than the horror stories I've heard from Josh. Of course, let's be honest here, Josh is kind of a wimp. The boy doesn't even drink soda because he claims the fizz hurts his tongue.

I glance up to look at Sam, who is watching Xander work with an expression of pride and immense respect. Then I look back to my wrist. I'm stunned to see that Xander is already finished with the first snowflake.

"That didn't take very long at all!" I remark.

33

"Nope. It's a pretty simple process," Xander says. "Now how about you, Morneau? Do I get to ink you up again any time soon?"

"I'm thinking about it," Sam admits. "Hers is looking great, man."

"Thank you. It is just... about... done!" he announces, wiping the excess ink and small drops of blood away from my wrist. "What do you think?"

"It's beautiful!" I exclaim. It really is. Intricate, classy, and a real work of art. Even if it is only two simple snowflakes. "Thank you so much, Xander."

"My pleasure Miss... I just realized I never got your name."

"It's Mel," I introduce myself as Xander applies a large bandage over my wrist.

"Well, nice to meet you, Miss Mel. Come back any time. Especially if you break up with your boyfriend." Xander winks again. I laugh.

"I'm hoping that's not going to happen. I kind of like this one."

"His girl's got a lot of spunk. He's a lucky guy. And Sam? I expect I'll see you before you go jetting off on your next tour. Even if it's not to get a tattoo."

"Absolutely, man. Thanks." And with that, Sam hands Xander a couple hundred dollar bills. "Keep the change."

"Have I ever told you you're my favorite client?"

"I'm everyone's favorite," Sam teases.

Before we leave, Xander instructs me to keep my bandage on for at least three hours. He also hands me a list of instructions on how to care for my new tattoo. Sam and I both thank him one final time before we exit out the back door and settle down inside Sam's car.

"Are you happy?" Sam asks me.

"I am. Thank you so much," I reply. No matter how many times I say it, I'm not sure he'll ever know just *how* happy he makes me.

"Good." Then, he takes my hand in his, turns it over, and pulls my wrist to his lips. "That will be a lot sexier when you don't have a bandage there."

I laugh and wrap my arms around him, pulling him into a kiss.

"I love you," I whisper in the safe sanctuary of that San Francisco alley.

"I love you too, Mel," Sam whispers back. "Happy Birthday."

CHAPTER 5

"Eleven minutes past the hour
I made a wish or two
Eleven hours still to go
Until my wish comes true
Eleven times eleven times
Something tells me that you knew
But girl, there's nothing more that I can do
Tonight I'm gonna wish for you..."

Song: "11:11"
Artist: The Kind of September
From: Untitled Future Album

So, my mom isn't particularly thrilled about the tattoo. Neither is my dad, but at least he acknowledges that I'm an adult - a twenty-one-year-old adult at that - and that what I do with my body is my decision. Brooklyn, on the other hand, loves my tattoo. She thinks it's just about the coolest thing ever and has already started designing her own for when she turns eighteen.

I thought that after what happened last week with those girls from her school, she'd be angry and upset with me.

But apparently, all three of the girls spread it around like wildfire that they got to meet Sam and Cory and that Brooklyn is actually like their little sister. In other words, Brooklyn is a very happy camper. She even made me a birthday card instead of going out and buying one like she usually does.

I spent my actual birthday celebrating with my family, but now, it's the day after and Joni and I are in town for a girls' afternoon before heading up to Sam's house for a supposedly low-key birthday party. The thing about Sam, though, is that he never does anything low-key. He is a go big or go home kind of guy.

In fact, I've got to be honest, I'm sort of wondering if maybe he paid Joni to take me out on this girls' afternoon. We just pulled up to a nail salon. Joni doesn't get manicures or pedicures. Ever. She thinks they're a waste of money.

"Why would I pay someone seventy dollars to paint my nails when I am perfectly capable of painting them myself?" she always asks.

I then argue that you also get really nice massages and bubbly foot baths included in that seventy dollars, but she usually ignores me.

"Are we going in here?" I ask her.

"Surprise!" she exclaims.

"But you hate mani-pedis," I remind her.

"I know, but it's your birthday. I wanted to do something special for you, remember?"

"Jo, you're the best!" I exclaim, throwing my arms around her.

"Well, you deserve it. You're my best friend and I want you to have a good birthday."

But the moment the words leave her lips, I feel a cold, gut-wrenching pang of guilt shoot down my chest and straight to my core. Joni is one of my best friends in the world, but how would she feel if she knew how much I was keeping from her? The secret relationship with Sam is one thing, but

37

covering up an affair between her ex-boyfriend and her twin brother's girlfriend? I might actually be the most horrible person to walk the face of the planet. Not that Joni cares for Tara at all. She actually despises her. But if the roles were reversed and she found out that someone close to me was being cheated on, I know she'd tell me.

I've told myself that over and over again. And yet, I still find myself shying away.

God, this *really* sucks.

While I wallow in shame and self-pity, Joni leads the way into the salon, where a pretty girl named Minsun tells us to pick out the nail polish we want and then to have a seat wherever we like. Joni picks a sensible crimson red and I decide on a pale winter blue.

As we settle into the comfy beige chairs, dipping our toes into the warm, bubbly water, the door to the salon opens and two girls who look to be around our age enter. It takes me a split second before I realize that I know them.

The shorter girl with big blue eyes and blonde hair is Samantha De Waal. She was in my English class in high school and probably one of the sweetest people I know. The tall, slender black girl is Kendra Jackson, our year's Valedictorian. I never had any classes with her, but I know that she was planning on studying aerospace engineering at CalTech.

"Hey! Mel! Joni!" Samantha waves and calls out to us.

"Samantha! Kendra! Wow, long time no see," Joni smiles back at them. "We would get up to greet you, but our feet are kind of wet."

"Why don't we come to you then?" Kendra asks as she and Samantha make their way over to see us. "How are you ladies?"

"We're great! How are you?" I ask.

"Good! Enjoying one last outing before I head back to school next week," Kendra explains.

"So soon?" Joni asks.

"Yeah. My job starts up a week before classes begin."

"What do you do?" I ask.

"I'm a Calculus tutor," she responds.

Okay, I feel like a bobble head doll right now. I barely even made it out of Pre-Cal in high school. I don't deserve to be in Kendra's presence, let alone having an actual conversation with her. She's *so* smart. But thing is, she's also really nice. Gorgeous, too. If the building rockets thing doesn't work out for her, she could definitely model.

"How about you, Samantha? What are you up to?" Joni asks.

"I'm studying literature at San Francisco State. I actually had two poems published in an anthology over the summer."

"Oh yeah! I think I saw something on Facebook about that. Congratulations," I tell her.

"Thanks," Samantha beams. "I guess you two are still doing the roadie thing."

"Guilty," I answer.

"That is *so* cool. I remember when they would sing at school assemblies. I just can't get over how far they've come," Kendra says.

"Right?" Samantha agrees. "No one ever believes me when I tell them I went to high school with The Kind of September."

"Speaking of, did I hear that you were dating a certain someone, Mel?" Kendra asks, a mischievous twinkle in her eye.

"What? No I'm not. I'm totally single. Why would you think that?" Yes, I am well aware that I look and sound as alarmed as I feel. But no one is supposed to know about Sam and me! No one is even supposed to suspect! What did Kendra hear? And who told her?

It's only after Joni tells them that it was just a stupid rumor spread by an equally stupid person that I realize

39

Kendra is referring to the false reports that I was dating The Kind of September's cute British boy, Oliver Berkley. I try not to breathe a sigh of relief. The rumors were quickly dispelled, but it appears a few people missed the memo.

"Well, I guess that's for the best. You guys work so closely, it might be weird," Samantha says.

"Yeah, totally." I hope I sound convincing.

"Anyway, I guess we should let you ladies enjoy the rest of your afternoon. It was nice to see you!" Kendra says. Then with one last wave, she and Samantha turn to head back to the waiting area.

"Kendra, Samantha, wait!" I call after them. They turn. "Are you guys doing anything tonight?"

"I don't think so," Kendra answers.

"Why don't you come to my birthday party? The guys will all be there. Well, except Oliver. He's still in England. But I'm sure the rest of them would love to see you and catch up."

"That's sweet, Mel, but we couldn't intrude," Samantha tells me.

"You're not intruding. I'm inviting you."

"Well, yeah, if you're sure! That sounds awesome!" Samantha replies, grinning with delight.

"Great! Give me your phone numbers and I'll text you the details. It's tonight at Sam's mom's house."

"Ugh, I cannot believe how gorgeous that boy grew up to be. He was such a bean pole in high school," Kendra laughs.

"He still is. He just hides it behind the tattoos and unwashed hair," Joni remarks.

"Hey, he might be the messiest human being alive, but he does wash his hair." I can't help it. I have to defend him. Personal hygiene is very important to Sam.

Okay, sort of. Personal hygiene is *sort of* important to him.

He'll at least shower before tonight.

I think.

"Speaking of tattoos," Joni comments once Samantha and Kendra disappear. She's giving me what Sam and Josh call the *evil eye* even though it's really just her raising an eyebrow.

"Yes?" I ask, feigning innocence.

"Sam sent my brother a Snapchat yesterday. Any ideas as to what it was?"

"Mars?"

"Cute," Joni deadpans. "Did you really get a tattoo?"

In response, I roll up my sleeve and expose my wrist. It's still a little tender, but it's healing nicely.

"Mel..." Joni groans.

"What? I wanted one. Besides, you can't even see it when I'm wearing sleeves."

"Well, what about when summer rolls around? What about bathing suit season, huh? You really want to be running around with... Are those snowflakes?"

"Yes. I think they're pretty."

"Why *snowflakes*? Oh, Mel, you are so going to regret this."

"Well, if I do, then I'm the one who has to live with it. Not you," I remind her.

"No, I'm the one who has to live with you having to live with it!"

"I'm not going to regret it," I assure her.

"You're only twenty. How could you possibly know that?"

"I'm twenty-*one* and I don't know how I know, I just do. I love my tattoo. I might even get another one someday!" I say that mostly just to horrify Joni even more than I already have, but to be honest, I wouldn't mind another. Not sure what I'll get or where I'd get it, but I'm open to the possibility.

Joni sighs. "Well, that's it. I've lost you. You've gone over to the dark side."

41

I don't believe this. Is she making jokes? Joni never makes jokes, or passes up the opportunity to give me a lecture on all the reasons why I'm wrong. Maybe she's giving me a break because it's my birthday.

"You know, you could get one too," I tell her as two women arrive to begin our pedicures.

"Don't push it, Mel," she warns me.

I wouldn't dream of it.

...

About two hours before the party is scheduled to begin, I receive a text from Sam.

Hey, I hate to ask this of you, but do you think you could come over a little early and help me set up?

I don't even have to think about it.

Of course, I reply. *When should I head over?*

Whenever you can.

I toss my makeup and party outfit into a backpack and head out almost immediately. I know it's my birthday and technically, I'm not supposed to be doing any work, but if Sam and his mom are nice enough to throw me a party, the least I can do is lend a hand to get everything together. Besides, their house is pretty huge.

After the guys really made it big, Sam moved his mother out of their tiny apartment in the city and into her dream house in Marin County. The house is brand new and very modern, with big open windows, a flat roof, and a balcony overlooking the exquisite backyard. Laurel loves hosting parties, although Sam has informed me that she's letting him have the run of the place tonight.

Sure enough, when I arrive, her car isn't parked in the driveway.

No wonder Sam needs help. Without Laurel there, he's in way over his head with the party planning.

I knock on the door, which Sam answers in a matter of seconds.

42

"Hey, birthday girl," he greets me with his usual megawatt smile. "Come on in."

I expect to step into a hopeless wreck of balloons, streamers, and maybe even unfolded laundry. Even though he's offered several times, Laurel refuses to let Sam hire a housekeeper. Let's face it, when he's not home, she probably doesn't need one.

But I'm stunned to find that the house looks good. It looks better than good. It looks ready-for-a-party good.

"Wait a minute, it looks great in here. Why do you need help setting up?" I ask, turning to look at him.

"I don't. I just wanted you all to myself for a little while," he grins. I can feel my cheeks beginning to glow pink as he wraps his arms around my waist and presses his forehead to mine.

"Well, you could have just told me that," I tell him.

"I could have, but I don't think it would have gotten you over here as fast," he teases me.

"You wanna bet?" I ask, rising up on my toes to kiss him.

In response, Sam wraps his arms around my waist and kisses me back with what I can only call absolute sincerity. His touch, his warm embrace, the way he seems to savor and absorb my kiss, everything within him and about him makes me feel loved. More than loved. Cherished.

And suddenly it's as if the rest of the world doesn't even exist.

After the kiss ends and the earth resumes its usual rotation, Sam looks down at me.

"I just realized something," he says with a playful smirk. I recognize the look. It's the same look he gets when he's come up with a joke that he thinks is clever but is actually just dumb.

"What's that?" I ask, not sure I really want to know the answer.

43

"You're officially twenty-one. I won't be twenty-one for another few months. That makes you older than me."

"Yes. Birthdays are tricky that way," I reply, wondering where he's going with this.

"Melissa Parker, you're a cougar!" Sam exclaims, sounding absolutely giddy.

I can feel my jaw drop.

"I am *not!*"

"You're an older woman dating a younger man. That is the definition of a cougar!"

"No, it is not!"

"It is. Look it up."

"No, I mean, I *know* it is, but they're talking about women who are like, twenty years older than their boyfriends. Not four months!"

"You can keep telling yourself that, Mel. I know that getting older can be a touchy subject for women your age," he grins.

"You know, you were so much more charming about thirty seconds ago."

"I'm sorry, I'm sorry." No he's not. He's far too amused. But being the mature older woman that I am, I decide to forgive him. He continues, "It's your birthday. Today is all about you." That's a little better.

He leads me into the living room, which, absent the clutter that seems to accompany Sam everywhere he goes, is even more bright and open than usual.

"Wow, it looks great in here. Laurel really outdid herself," I say.

"Why do you assume that my mom did all the work? Don't you think I wanted to help make the house look nice for my girlfriend's birthday?" Sam asks.

"Aw, you actually cleaned?"

"I'll have you know I picked up two pairs of shoes and carried them all the way to my bedroom."

"Wow, what a stud." I laugh.

44

"Okay, if I'm being honest, my mom did do most of the cleaning," Sam confesses. "But that was only because I had a few last minute birthday errands to run."

"Oh, really?" I ask.

"Yep. Speaking of which... Do you want to see another one of your presents?"

"What? Sam, you already got me my present. Remember?"

"I know, but I wanted to surprise you," he tells me. Then, *much* to my surprise, he lifts up his shirt and pulls down the waistband on his jeans. I'm about to ask exactly *what* he thinks he's doing when I see it: a brand new tattoo, identical to mine.

"Sam..."

"I would have put it on my wrist, but I didn't have any room," he says. "Besides, I figured it was best to keep it hidden. If word got out that we had matching tattoos, people might get suspicious." He has a point.

"What about Xander? Did you tell him?"

"No. Just told him that I liked your tattoo and wanted the same design. If anything, he thinks that I'm into you and trying to woo you."

I laugh. "Does he really think that would work?"

"Of course, it's Xander. That's how he operates. He woos with tattoos." And with that, Sam grabs me by the waist and dips me backwards, just like a dancer might dip his partner at the end of a Tango. "So... is it working?"

I don't know why he has to ask.

CHAPTER 6

"I've been told that life is more than
Faces that we see
But I've been wondering what you think of
When you look at me
I know that nothing lasts forever
But you and me together
We might be something kind of wonderful..."

Song: "Kind of Wonderful"
Artist: The Kind of September
From the Album: *Meet Me on the Midway*

Joni and Cory arrive shortly before the party begins at eight o'clock.

"Happy birthday!" Cory greets me with a one-armed hug. He's carrying two brown bags, the contents of which are clinking. "We come bearing booze!"

"And cake," Joni adds, holding up a large box.

"Ooh, I'll take that!" Sam jokes, shoving Cory aside to get a glimpse of the tantalizing frosted sweetness that is my birthday cake. He and I have both changed clothes since I arrived earlier. I'm in a white skirt and turquoise top,

46

accentuated with gold jewelry. Sam, never one to pass up an opportunity to look ridiculously attractive, is wearing black jeans and gray-and-black-striped button down shirt. He's also wearing his Old Spice cologne. He knows it's my favorite.

"Not a chance, you bottomless sugar pit," Joni snaps, slipping past Sam and into the house. I can't help but notice how pretty she looks. Of course, Joni always looks absolutely gorgeous with her thick brown hair and big green eyes, but tonight, in her stylish blue pin skirt and sleeveless white blouse, she looks particularly stunning. Cory, on the other hand, looks just the same as he always does; tall and lanky with a messy mop of brown hair and dressed in jeans and an old band t-shirt.

"By the way, Sam, did you get the text that Oliver came home early?" Cory asks.

"No. But then, I haven't checked my phone in about three hours. In fact, now that you mention it, I'm not actually sure I know where my phone is..." Sam remarks, glancing back at me as though I can magically point him in the direction of his lost phone.

If I had to guess, it's probably lost somewhere in the depths of the couch. That's where we spent the better part of the last three hours. Of course, I'm not going to say that out loud in front of Joni and Cory. Instead, I offer to call it.

"So, who else is coming tonight?" Joni asks Sam after setting the cake (which, apparently, I'm not allowed to see until it's actually time to cut it) in the kitchen.

"Just the guys, the band, and a few friends from the area. Mel told me that you ran into Samantha and Kendra from high school. Oh! And Morning Muses!"

"Really?" I ask.

Morning Muses is an up-and-coming local band, though the guys actually heard them for the first time over the summer at a music festival in North Carolina. Even though their stylings are on totally different ends of the

47

musical spectrum, they really hit it off. Before the end of the festival, The Kind of September had a brand new opening act for their next world tour. I've only met them a couple of times, but they seem like a really cool group. I'm thrilled that they want to come to my birthday party.

"Yeah. I hope you don't mind. Josh is actually the one who invited them. But I think it will be a good opportunity for all of us to hang out a bit before the tour kicks off," Sam answers.

"That sounds awesome! I'm excited to get to know them better," I tell him. I kind of wish I'd known they were coming earlier, though. I would have made more of an effort to actually listen to their album.

Unlike The Kind of September, Morning Muses play their own instruments. They're not pop like the guys, but they're not full blown rock and roll, either. Joni refers to them as Punk-Pop. They have four members: Toby Millard, Jefferson Flynn, Kaveh Izadi, and Ashalyn Zimerman, all of whom are around our age, maybe a year or two younger.

As if on cue, the doorbell rings and Josh arrives, accompanied by Toby, Kaveh, and Ashalyn.

"There's the birthday girl!" Josh exclaims and pulls me into a huge hug. Although I will always prefer Sam's embrace to anyone's, Josh gives pretty excellent hugs. He also gives me a big kiss right on the cheek. With blond hair, big brown eyes, and a smile that could probably melt the snowflakes right off my wrist, Josh is widely considered the cutest member of the Kind of September. He knows it, too. "So, what's it like?" he asks me. "The big two-one? You feeling over the hill yet?"

"Hardly!" I laugh. Along with being The Cute One, Josh is also the youngest member of the group and he is *constantly* rubbing it in our faces. It used to be kind of funny back when he was the only one who couldn't get into R-rated movies, but now the laugh's on the rest of us.

"Just wait till those gray hairs start popping up. Youth is a fleeting gift, Mel. Cherish it," he teases me.

"I'll keep that in mind," I remark before finally turning to greet his friends. "Hi. I'm Melissa. I think we've met maybe once or twice."

"Yeah, it's nice to see you again. Happy Birthday!" Ashalyn says. She looks so much like a girl in a punk band. Her black hair, which she's wearing tied up in a ponytail, is streaked with purple and blue, and she has a nose ring. Her black jeans are ripped and she's wearing layered black and white tank tops. Despite her hardcore appearance, however, she seems very open and friendly and even though I already know that she is about a thousand times cooler than I will ever be, I think Ashalyn and I might just hit it off.

"Oh, right! Introductions!" Josh says. "Mel, this is Ashalyn, Toby, and Kaveh. Jeff wanted to come, but he's got food poisoning."

"Ew, gross," I cringe. I remember when Sam had food poisoning in high school. It was the only time in my life I wasn't able to make him smile. He was just that miserable.

"Well, that's what he gets for eating raw squid," Kaveh remarks. He's very handsome, with thick dark hair that falls across his forehead and ever so slightly into his big dark eyes, and the beginnings of a beard. I imagine Sam and Josh are both jealous of his ability to grow fantastic facial hair.

Toby, the group's drummer, doesn't say much. That strikes me as kind of odd because I feel like most drummers I've met (not that I've met all that many) have really exuberant personalities. Maybe he's just shy. The guys' drummer, Chris Ortega, is one of the most outgoing guys you'll ever meet. Of course, every time I mention how open and friendly he is, Sam falls back into his old *Mel has a thing for drummers* routine. I don't know why he thinks that's so funny. Thankfully, I haven't heard that joke since we started dating. Maybe our relationship has put an end to my alleged drummer infatuation once and for all.

49

God, I hope so.

Kendra and Samantha are the next to arrive, followed shortly by Chris and two other members of the guys' band, Neil and Anthony. Then Oliver shows up, looking adorable in blue jeans and a brand new knit sweater vest. His curly brown hair is a bit longer than usual and I can't help but notice that he looks healthier than he did the last time I saw him. A few weeks of hearty, home-cooked meals must have done him good.

"Happy Birthday, Mel." He greets me with a swift hug and hands me a small gift bag.

"Thank you! I'm glad you could make it tonight! Did you have a good Christmas?" I ask him.

"I did. Very quiet, which was a nice change."

"I feel you," I grin as Sam appears by my side.

"Oliver! Good to see you, man!"

"You as well, Morneau. I take it life's been treating you well these last few weeks?"

"Oliver, my brother, life is treating me like a king."

I can't help it. I smile.

"Glad to hear it," Oliver says, but he's no longer paying any attention to us. His eyes have drifted across the room to where Joni stands, laughing with Kendra and Samantha.

I'd suspected for a while that Oliver had a crush on Joni, but ever since he confessed it to me last month, he'd become much less subtle about it. That, or I was just picking up on it more now that I knew for sure.

"Okay, you've got to tell me honestly," Sam murmurs to me once Oliver is out of earshot. "Joni's never said anything to you about Oliver?"

"Not a word," I answer truthfully.

"But she's got to know. The poor guy is an open book."

Part of me is inclined to agree with him. After all, Joni is one of the smartest people I know. But on the other hand, her self-esteem took a major blow after Jesse broke up with

50

her. It's possible that she doesn't see the way that Oliver looks at her simply because, in a way, she can't. As her friend, it's very disheartening to know that Joni doesn't think very much of herself. We all think the world of her. Even Jesse.

Speaking of, I can't help but notice he's the only guest who hasn't arrived yet. Is it too much to hope that maybe he's going to bail out at the last minute? I know I'm going to have to face him sometime, but why does it have to be tonight? It's my birthday party. I'm supposed to be happy tonight. And looking Jesse Scott in his lying, cheating, secretive eyes is simply not going to make me happy.

And of course, the doorbell just rang.

Happy birthday to me.

I think about sneaking off to join the rest of the girls while Sam answers the door. After all, if I'm around Joni, maybe Jesse will be less inclined to approach me. But we're going to run into each other sooner or later. Might as well get it over with.

"Hey, Sam. Sorry I'm a little late," Jesse apologizes, stepping through the doorway.

Physically, Jesse is one the sexiest guys to walk the face of the planet. He's tall, he's fit, he has big blue eyes in which many girls have found themselves lost, and his auburn hair is always perfectly disheveled, like he just rolled out of bed, but in a very attractive way. Jesse is the band's proverbial bad boy and he definitely likes to look the part.

And as it turns out, he likes to act the part as well.

"What? Thirty minutes? I'd say this is early for you," Sam jokes. Jesse isn't exactly known for his punctuality.

"Touché," Jesse grins. Then he finally turns to me. "Happy birthday, Melissa."

"Thank you." My reply is rather stiff. I can hear it. I know Jesse can hear it. I only hope that Sam can't. Fortunately, Jesse isn't much of a hugger, so I get to bypass the painfully awkward birthday embrace.

"So... everybody here?" Jesse asks.

51

Okay. Sam is definitely going to know something is up. Jesse never makes small talk. He says what he needs to say and then goes about his business. He's also visibly nervous. Or maybe that's just me.

Is it hot in here?

But Sam, God bless him, just smiles and answers, "Yep, we're all waiting on you. So come in, mingle, join the party."

"Thanks. I think I will."

And just like that, he's gone. It takes every ounce of strength that I possess to not breathe a sigh of relief.

Sam, meanwhile, slips a coy hand around the small of my back and smiles. "Well, the gang's all here!" he announces. "Do you want to cut the cake? Or just enjoy the evening for a bit?"

"I'm inclined to say let's just enjoy the evening, but you really want a piece of that cake, don't you?" I ask. I know him too well.

"I know this is the part where I'm supposed to say something romantic like 'no pastry could be sweeter than your face' but, yes. Yes, I want cake. I need cake. Cake is my second true love. After you."

"Well, at least that's more romantic than that pastry line you just came up with," I laugh. "Let's go cut the cake."

"You are my favorite," he says, planting a swift kiss on my cheek. "But first, we have to sing 'Happy Birthday!' Come on!"

I've said it before and I'll say it again: Sam is easily the most enthusiastic person I know. He finds enjoyment in everything that life has to offer. It's one of my very favorite things about him.

While he runs around, instructing people to congregate in the kitchen, I linger back, wondering where I need to be. Tragically, this leaves me open and available to unwanted attention.

"Melissa," Jesse greets me again. Why can't he just call me Mel? Everyone else does. "So, how've you been?"

I don't care for his beating around the bush nonsense. I mean, to be fair, I do it all the time. But I know that Jesse doesn't care how I've been and he knows that I know. So instead of playing along, I reply, "No, Jesse, I haven't told anyone."

"Well, nothing like cutting to the chase," he comments and shoves his hands into his pockets.

"Look, it's my birthday. Do we really need to do this tonight?"

"Better tonight than when Tara's around."

"Is that what you think? That I'm going to rat the two of you out to Cory? Or is that what *she* thinks?" I demand. The look on Jesse's face says it all. "Well, you can tell her that she has nothing to worry about. If I was going to tattle on the two of you, I would have done so already."

"Thank you, Melissa." Jesse pats me on the shoulder. For some reason, his words infuriate me.

"Oh, don't you *dare* thank me," I hiss. "I'm not doing this for either of you. I'm doing it for the rest of the group. Because it's none of my business. And because I don't want to see a good thing fall apart."

"And we don't either. It's the last thing that we want," he assures me. "I just wish there was a way out of this without hurting anyone's feelings."

"Well, that's not going to happen," I snap. Seriously, I don't know what's gotten into me. I'm rarely confrontational and I'm never this aggressive. Well, Sam might tell you otherwise, but he means it as a compliment. The point is this whole mess with Jesse and Tara is bringing out a whole new side of me and I don't think I like it.

"I know," Jesse sighs. "Anyway, I just wanted to clear the air. You've been a good friend to me and I haven't always returned the favor. I know I've put you in a tight situation, and I'm sorry. We really never meant for anyone else to get involved."

"Thanks, Jesse."

It doesn't make everything all better, but at least he's acknowledging it. Maybe Jesse and I can go back to the way we were before. Maybe it doesn't have to be as awkward and uncomfortable as I'd originally feared.

"Mel!" Kendra exclaims, appearing behind me. "Is it my imagination or were you just getting cozy with *Jesse Scott?!*"

Or maybe it will be worse.

CHAPTER 7

"Why do you keep asking me
If I'm alright
Oh, can't you see
I don't have time to make believe
That everything is what it seems
What do you think?
What do you think?"

Song: "What Do You Think"
Artist: Morning Muses
From the Album: *Nightfall*

Three new rumors began circulating around online in the early morning hours following my birthday party. One of them claims that Sam has a new secret sweetheart in the Bay Area. Another states that this new romance is actually an old flame from high school. Several sources are even claiming to know the identity of Sam's mystery girl: the beautiful and brilliant CalTech engineer, Kendra Jackson.

I feel so bad. Her name has been trending on various social media sites ever since. I've tried texting her a few times to apologize for the mess. After all, I was the one who invited her to the party in the first place. But she keeps assuring me that it's not bothering her and that she's not even on Twitter and that she's certain that it will all die down within a week or so. I hope she's right. Some of the things that the fans are saying about her are downright abusive.

The second rumor flying hot off the press is that Oliver and I have rekindled our star-crossed romance. That's right. For one reason or another, #*Meliver* refuses to die. I have no idea why. Oliver barely spoke to me all night. True, he did bring me back a scarf from England, but does no one remember the beautiful and very expensive birthstone necklace that he bought for Joni last month? Come on, people. Oliver has *never* given me jewelry. Come to think of it, my actual boyfriend has never given me jewelry either. Unless you count those TKOS earrings, which I really don't.

I guess if gossip is going to spread, I'd rather it be this and not, say, the actual truth. I just wish I understood how these stories manifest in the first place. Where do they come from? I mean, I know the guys are stalked by the paparazzi on a near-constant basis, but to be able to identify Kendra as being at my birthday party? That's just downright creepy. There must be an inside source, but the only person I know who would willingly sell us out to the press was mercifully absent last night. Of course, I'm talking about Tara.

Which brings me to Rumor Number Three. It would appear that the resurgence of #*Meliver* comes with a new, drama-infused love triangle. From what I can gather, there's a source out there claiming that another member of the band has feelings for me even though I'm "with" Oliver. That member just happens to be the one and only Jesse Scott.

And that, my friends, is irony at its finest.

I know you're never supposed to read gossip articles, especially those written about *you*, but curiosity and masochism apparently go hand-in-hand. The reports I've scoured so far mostly say the same thing: Oliver and I have been quietly dating for months. Then, when he went back to England, Jesse developed feelings for me, which he professed at my birthday party. Now there's a "rift" between Oliver and Jesse and The Kind of September's entire tour might be cancelled and the band is probably going to break up any day now. Meanwhile, I'm watching from the sidelines, trying to decide if I want to stay with my sweet British heartthrob or if I want to throw it all away for a shot at saving bad boy Jesse from his dark, broody ways.

This is ridiculous. If my name is going to be popping up in the tabloids this much, I might as well just come out and admit that I am, in fact, dating a member of the band, just not the one that everyone thinks. The only problem is once I do that, it's out there for good. Right now, it's just speculation and stupid gossip that, as Kendra pointed out, will probably fade within a week or so. Irritating, but not permanent. I can't help but wonder though, why is it always me? Joni is around the guys just as much as I am. She even publicly dated one of them. Why isn't anyone spreading rumors that she's having a torrid affair with Josh?

Probably because no one would actually buy it. Even the media knows how professional and uptight Joni can be. She's also very open about her online and media presence. I'm more private. All of my social media profiles are locked and secured. Maybe that makes me seem like I've got something to hide. I'm not sure. Whatever the reason, I'm not going to start sharing my personal life now. Somehow, I can't help but feel that would make everything worse.

Oh, and for the record, in spite of what he wants everyone to think, Jesse is neither dark nor broody.

...

Now that my birthday is over, it's time to get back into the swing of things. Rehearsals for the Meet Me on the Midway Tour begin in just a few short weeks, but first, we're flying out to New York. The guys are performing in the annual New Year's Eve celebration at Times Square. It's all

57

very exciting. True, we've all been to New York at least half a dozen times by now, but never on New Year's Eve. Joni even texted me last night to ask what I was going to wear for the event. I still haven't figured that one out. I packed five potential outfits: three dresses, two sweaters, three different coats, and two scarves. To be honest though, my final decision will probably end up being made based on how cold it is outside. I may be in love with the idea of winter, but I'm kind of a wimp when it actually comes to frigid temperatures.

After we arrive in New York, we have about an hour of downtime before we head out to the Square for sound check. While the guys warm up and rehearse their set list for tonight, I'm making sure my trusty camera batteries are charged, polishing my lenses, and double checking the space available on all five of my memory cards. I haven't photographed a show since the guys performed on *Good Morning America* last month and this one is going to be huge. Not because it's a particularly long set, but because of the occasion and the venue. I'd love to try to get some shots of the Square as well, especially when the countdown to midnight begins, but I'm not sure if that will be possible.

We'll see.

No matter what, I make a mental note to stay as far away from both Oliver and Jesse as possible. With all the paparazzi and news crews and bloggers the place will be crawling with tonight, the last thing any of us needs is photographic evidence that I'm involved with either of them. Chances are I won't get to see any of the guys, not even Sam, until after the ball has dropped, so there's really nothing to worry about. Still. I like to be prepared.

By three in the afternoon, the streets surrounding Times Square are completely blocked off and crowds are already beginning to assemble.

"Now *this* is going to be a dream come true," Sam remarks, chancing a peek around one of the curtains and out to the gathering audience. "Do you know how long I've wanted to celebrate New Year's Eve in Times Square?"

"*And* you get to perform," I remind him.

"Yeah, that's pretty cool too. But just the chance to actually be here! To see it all in person! Who knows? Maybe I'll even get to kiss my favorite girl at midnight..." he murmurs, slipping sly fingers in between mine. I blush.

"And just how do you expect to pull that off?" I ask. Not that I'm opposed. I'm actually all for it. I'm just not sure it will be possible.

"I have my ways," he winks. Then he catches a glimpse of something over my shoulder. "Well, look who it is."

I turn, expecting to see someone good. My stomach drops down to my feet, though, when I find myself exchanging extremely uncomfortable glances with a tall, blonde beauty in a bright magenta coat.

Tara Meeks.

"I didn't know *she* was supposed to be here!" I gasp.

"She probably flew in to surprise Cory," Sam tells me before he's called back for one final mic check.

Sure enough, a few moments later, Cory has swept her up in his arms and is kissing her like Ryan Gosling might kiss one of his onscreen leading ladies. That is if Ryan Gosling were really tall and lanky and kind of had hair like a cartoon character.

Wow. Why doesn't Sam kiss me like that?

Meanwhile, I can't help but notice Jesse trying not to watch from the sidelines. Granted, he's much subtler than I am, openly gawking as though I'm anticipating an actual train wreck rather than a metaphorical one. I expect Joni to come marching up to me at any moment, bemoaning her existence and questioning the very merit of the universe, but she's nowhere to be seen. That's probably a good thing.

I hope that Tara will take a chapter from Joni's book and disappear quickly as well. Unfortunately, that doesn't happen. As soon as Cory releases her from his embrace, she waltzes directly over to me, hair dancing behind her, and arms outreached.

"Mel!" she exclaims, greeting me like a long lost sister. "It's so good to see you! Did you have a good Christmas?"

"What are you doing?" I ask. I'm not going to lie to you. I'm a little scared right now.

"What are you talking about?"

"You can drop the charade, Tara. I promise, I'm not going to tell anyone."

"This isn't a charade. You're my friend. I'm happy to see you."

Since when? I want to ask. Instead, I force back a grimace and say, "Well, thank you. That's very nice. But you might want to dial it back just a bit if you don't want people getting suspicious."

Tara sighs. "Okay, fine. I get it. No more mushy stuff. But Mel, in all seriousness, if there is ever anything I can do for you, just let me know. Like, your hair. You know, with some highlights and someone to teach how to do your makeup, you'd actually be really pretty." Suddenly, she gasps. "I could give you a full makeover!"

I try to smile. Really, I do. But I think I just end up looking like I'm trying not to throw up.

"You know, Tara, as fun as that sounds, I just - I really don't have time for that."

"Oh, come on. Why not? We could have a girls' night! And who knows? Maybe with a little help from yours truly, Oliver would notice you for real."

And the fun just keeps on coming.

"Tara. Thank you. But for the last time, there is nothing going on with me and Oliver. Or any of the guys, for that matter." Okay, that lie came out a little feebly, but I don't think Tara noticed.

"Suit yourself. All I'm saying is I could help you out a lot, Mel. Just think about it."

60

And with that, she flounces away, leaving me alone and wondering what in the world just happened.

...

The show goes off without a hitch. As always, the guys are spectacular. I managed to get some great photographs. Though there were a few moments I had to remind myself to shoot the other guys too, not just Sam. Sometimes, he just makes it so difficult to concentrate! Dancing around in his black skinny jeans and sexy designer jacket, with his dark blond locks styled to perfection and falling gracefully into those big blue eyes...

What was I saying?

Oh, right. The show. It was perfect. The fans were as enthusiastic and adoring as ever. The guys performed all the singles off the new album as well as a few of their older hits. The aesthetics, too, were absolutely breathtaking. The lighting crew really outdid themselves with a spectacular display of blue, yellow, red, and violet strobes and lasers. Now, the guys are doing a post-show interview with one of the news stations broadcasting the event while I do my best not to get lost in all the excitement. And in the colorful, chaotic, and quite frankly, dizzying crowds.

"Welcome, guys! Great show! You all just have so much energy! I don't see how you do it," the man holding the microphone says. I realize that I recognize his face, but I couldn't tell you his name.

"Lots of coffee," Jesse grins.

"That, and I think the fans have a lot to do with it," Oliver elaborates.

"It's true," Sam agrees. "When you're up there with your friends and with the people you love most in the world watching you... It's impossible to not feel that high. That energy."

"Excellent, excellent. That is so sweet," the reporter says. "Tell me, what does it feel like, knowing that just a short time ago, you were five normal guys, and now you're here, performing at one of the biggest New Year's Eve extravaganzas in the world?"

"Unreal. Absolutely unreal," Josh answers.

"We absolutely realize how lucky we are to have made it here and we really owe it all to the fans and to our amazing crew, our band... We definitely wouldn't be here without any of them," Cory says.

"One last question. There's been a lot of talk recently about the ladies in your lives. Are any of you planning on a New Year's kiss?" the reporter asks.

"I am," Cory grins. "My beautiful, amazing, wonderful girlfriend flew all the way out from LA to support us."

"Isn't that romantic. Anyone else?" the reporter wonders, glancing at the rest of the guys.

"I'll be locking lips with a piece of pizza. Does that count?" Josh asks.

"Not quite," the reporter tells him.

And that is how you effectively end an on-air interview with one of the most prominent news station in the country.

After the guys disperse, I stick close to Joni for the remainder of the evening, though I can't help but notice she keeps glancing around, like she's hoping to dodge something. Or someone.

"You okay?" I ask her.

"Yeah. I just don't want to accidentally see that blonde-haired harpy making out with my brother on camera," she mutters.

"Ugh. Do you think she would?"

Joni gives me her trademark *you actually have to ask?* glance in response. In this case, it is totally warranted.

At about ten minutes till midnight, Sam appears out of nowhere, grabs my wrist, and says, "Hey! Come here! I need to show you something." Then he drags me off without even a farewell to Joni.

He leads me back to a dark, isolated hallway backstage. It almost looks like a storage area.

"Are you sure we're allowed to be back here?"

"No," he answers with a cheeky grin. Then, he pulls me into his arms, brushes my hair away from my face, and tilts my face up towards his. "Happy New Year." And then he's kissing me. And it's bliss.

How is he so good at this? I've been kissing him for over a month now and his touch still sends my spirit soaring and my heart into a frenzy. High off his kiss, his embrace, his very presence, I pull him closer, savoring the feel of his firm, slender body up against mine.

"Happy New Year to you," I whisper once we've finally broken apart. "But it isn't midnight yet, is it?"

"No, we've still got about three minutes. I thought it might be selfish of me to drag you off into the shadows, away from the celebration. I wanted my New Year's kiss, but I also want to make sure you're back in time to see the ball drop and experience ringing in the New Year in the actual Square."

"Sam..." I don't know what to say. Sam Morneau can be loud and goofy and yeah, sometimes he forgets to wash his socks, but he is also one of the most genuine and thoughtful people I've ever known. To prove it, I rise up and kiss him swiftly on the lips. "I love you."

"I love you too, Mel. This is going to be the best year of our lives. I can feel it."

"I can, too."

We make it back out to the Square just in time for the countdown to begin. It's incredible, to be there in the middle of a scene I've witnessed so many times before from my television screen. The energy in the air is electrifying. Everyone surrounding us is alive with the hope and promise and joy of a brand new year. Every light seems to shimmer with that same sense of magic.

And as the Times Square Ball reaches its mark and the lights of the new year blaze to life and the crowds burst into cheers and a chorus of "Auld Lang Syne," I know, deep in my heart, that Sam is right. This is going to be the best year of our lives. Come what may.

CHAPTER 8

"I give to you the memories
Of silver stars and stormy seas
Of music and of clarity
I give it all to you
If I could give the memory
Of just how much you mean to me
You'd never be left wondering
I give to you
Yeah I give to you..."

Song: "My Gift"
Artist: The Kind of September
From the Album: *Meet Me on the Midway*

A week has passed since New Year's Eve and we're on our way to Los Angeles. As always, it was hard to say goodbye to my family, but I'm also eager and excited for the new tour season to begin. The guys will have three weeks of rigorous rehearsals in January, one week of down time at the beginning of February, and then three weeks of interviews and guest appearances before the tour officially kicks off at the beginning of March. We'll be in the States until the end of July, and then we head overseas to a number of countries in Europe and Asia, where we'll be until mid-October.

But I'm getting way ahead of myself. First, we have to get through these rehearsals. And by "we" I mean I. *I* have to get through these rehearsals. True, I won't be singing ten hours a day or dancing until my feet fall off, but I will be doing everything within my power to avoid in-depth conversations with Cory, awkward run-ins with Jesse, and any ill-conceived attempts to bribe my already-guaranteed silence from Tara.

She already has Joni asking questions about the inordinate amount of tweets and Facebook posts she tags me in. I made the mistake of adding her as a friend back when she and Cory first got together. That was before I knew that she was going to end up being a total flake and cheating on my friend. I thought about un-friending her after I walked in on her and Jesse, but then I realized it might look suspicious if I deleted her out of the blue, especially when I hadn't taken the time to do so before, like after the huge fight we had back in November. Long story short, she's the one who started the rumor that Oliver and I were dating, I called her a few mean names, it was your typical middle school spat. Except one of us is a semi-famous model. And the other one is me.

Simply put, it just doesn't make sense, after everything that's happened, for Tara to suddenly think of me as her new BFF. Joni is well aware of this and, as my actual BFF, has every right to be suspicious.

It's a little sad though, when you think about it. Tara isn't acting out of a guilty conscience. She's being overly friendly because she thinks I'm going to out her and Jesse, or possibly even blackmail her. Now, I'm not that kind of person, but I can't help but wonder if maybe all of the other people in Tara's life are. Why else would she assume that of someone she barely even knows?

Thankfully, I've come up with a moderately believable explanation as to why Tara is suddenly acting like we're grand old chums. I told Joni that Tara still really wants to hook her best friend up with Sam and for some reason, she thinks that being extra nice to me will sway him. Granted, it's just one more lie to pile onto an ever-growing heap, which isn't great, but what else can I do?

I guess I could tell her the truth, but at this point, I'm afraid I'm in too deep. I feel like confessing would just make everything worse. So I'm going to keep my mouth shut and let the chips fall where they may. I only hope I don't live to regret my decision.

Or should I say my cowardice.

...

Tonight is our first night in LA. The guys start rehearsals first thing in the morning, so naturally we're all wide awake at eleven o'clock at night, eating pizza, and playing one of the most pathetic games of poker the state of California has ever seen in Josh, Jesse, and Oliver's hotel room. I'm not playing, partly because for the life of me, I can't grasp the rules, and partly because I have no poker face. Ironic, considering just how many secrets I'm keeping under wraps, but the fact still stands.

As far as the game goes, Joni is absolutely slaughtering the guys. Cory is trailing at a distant second, with Sam and Jesse pretty much tied for last. Oliver cashed out a few rounds back and settled down on the sofa with his laptop, and although Josh put up a valiant fight, Joni wiped him clean, so he's currently sitting in the corner of the room, shirtless, strumming on Jesse's guitar, and eating the remaining pizza straight out of the box. He's also wearing my sunglasses.

I've probably said it before, but Josh definitely dances to the beat of his own drum. Except his drum is something more like an empty coffee can.

"Why did I agree to this again?" Jesse groans as Joni wins yet another round, which included the last of his green chips. To be honest, I'm not sure how much those are worth, but if the look on his face is any indication, he wanted to hold on to them. You know, you'd think that losing a few green poker chips wouldn't be that big a deal for one of the richest guys under twenty-five on the planet.

"I have no idea. How many times have we lost to her since high school?" Sam wonders, slapping a card down onto the table.

Maybe that's it. Maybe Jesse just doesn't like to lose. More specifically, maybe he just doesn't like to lose to Joni. I can't help but notice that whenever Cory wins a round, Jesse doesn't complain at all. In fact, he's even congratulated Cory on a few hands. But then, that could be his guilt manifesting. *Sorry I'm hooking up with your girlfriend behind your back, Pal. But hey, you're a great poker player!*

"Too many," Jesse grumbles, laying down his hand. "Hey! Look at that! I won! In your face, bitches!" Joni throws him a glare. "And I mean that in the most respectful way possible."

Sam, however, heaves a sigh. "That's it. I'm cashing out."

"What? No, come on! The game is just getting started!" Jesse exclaims, stacking his newly acquired chips into neat, color-coded piles.

"Exactly. And I'm exhausted."

"I'll play for you, Sam!" Josh calls. I think he really wants another chance to salvage what remains of his dignity.

"You're going to lose everything," Oliver warns Sam.

"Oh, what the heck? Go for it, Josiah," Sam says.

Josh lets out a victorious whoop and darts across the room without bothering to grab his shirt or wipe the pizza sauce off his chin.

"Alright! The Josh-Meister is back in the game!" he exclaims.

"The Josh-Meister?" I can't help it. I have to ask.

"Oh, please don't tell me that's going to be a thing now," Oliver remarks dryly.

"What, you don't like the new nickname, Oliverocious?" Josh asks.

"I'm not even sure what that's supposed to mean."

"It's a combination of Oliver and ferocious. Seriously, you don't get that?"

"No one gets you, Josh," Joni comments, dealing out a new hand.

"Josh's Angels do!" Josh remind her.

Quick backstory: Josh's Angels are what the sub-group of The Kind of September fans who are totally devoted to Josh now call themselves. A few weeks ago, Josh made the offhanded comment on Twitter that after he retired from the music industry, he was going to become the next Charlie, like from *Charlie's Angels*. This led to self-professed "Josh Girls" from all over the world pledging themselves to him and rechristening themselves as Josh's Angels.

I'm really glad none of us were around him the day #JoshsAngels went viral and topped the trending topics on social media. The texts alone were unbearable enough.

"Josh's Angels are their own kind of special," Jesse mutters.

"If by special you mean brilliant with exquisite taste in men, then yes, I'd have to agree with you," Josh smiles.

While our friends continue their game, Sam glances over to me with sleepy eyes and gives a slight nod toward the door. I hope no one can see me blushing.

"I think I'm going to call it a night," I announce, rising up out of my chair.

"I'm right there with you," Sam agrees. "I'll walk you back to your room."

Usually, Josh would take this as an opportunity to make a sleazy remark about how we always seem to sneak off together at the same time, but he's too engrossed in the game to care.

Everyone bids us a distracted goodnight as Sam and I slip out of the room and into the hallway. Sam immediately laces his fingers through mine.

"Are you okay?" he asks. That surprises me.

"Yes," I answer. "Why? Do I not seem okay?"

"You seem pensive," he responds. "Is something on your mind?"

"Nothing really in particular. I guess I'm just thinking about how it's all getting ready to start again. And it's exciting. But it's also a little overwhelming."

"I hear you," he says, pulling me into his arms in the middle of the hallway. "But it's all going to be totally and completely, blow-your-mind amazing."

"I know," I smile up at him as he gently kisses my forehead, then my eyelid, and finally my lips. I lose myself in his embrace until a thought occurs to me. "You know, there are probably security cameras out here."

"Then maybe we should take this little rendezvous to a more private location," Sam murmurs against my temple. I'm all for that. "Do you want to go back to my room? I actually have one more belated birthday present for you."

"Another one? Sam, you already got a tattoo for me."

"I know, I know. But this one didn't cost anything, I promise. I would have had it ready for you on your actual birthday, but I wanted it to be perfect."

"You do realize that you're going to spoil me, right?" I ask him.

"That's the plan," he winks.

He leads me to the room that he and Cory are sharing and sits me down on the bed. Then, he disappears into the closet and begins digging around for something. While I wait, I take in the details of the room. This is probably the nicest hotel we've ever stayed in. Our suites are more like miniature apartments since we'll be here for an extended period of time. Each room has a couch, a kitchen, a small

70

dining area, and a spectacular view of Los Angeles. Sam and Cory even have a clear view of the Hollywood sign.

Seriously, who would have thought we'd end up here?

"Okay, you have to promise not to laugh," Sam says, emerging from the closet carrying a brand new acoustic guitar.

"When did you get that?" I ask him.

"Little Christmas present I bought myself. Jesse has been kind of teaching me to play here and there. Over the break, I decided it was time to really get serious about it."

"Sam! I can't believe you didn't tell me!" I exclaim. God, he looks so good holding a guitar.

"Well, I wasn't sure I'd actually be any good," Sam laughs. "I'm definitely not as good as Jesse or any of the guys in the band, but I did manage to pick out a new tune that I think might work for our next album. Do you want to hear it?"

"Yes," I whisper, grinning from ear to ear.

"Alright. Here it goes. I don't have a name for it yet, and you know, it will sound much better with someone else playing it and all the guys singing, but I wanted you to be the first one to hear it."

I'm already fighting back tears when he begins to play, his long fingers gliding gracefully across the strings. His new melody is gentle and sincere, like springtime in a song.

Then he closes his eyes and begins to sing.

Remember the first day you smiled at me?
The stars were in your eyes,
In fields of diamonds and fireflies.
Remember those sweet moments of innocence...
Of sandcastles and seas of blue,
Just like this world was made for two,
Just like my heart was meant for you.

And why did it take me so long

To make your love a song?
And why did it take so long to see
What was right in front of me?
I'm never gonna let you go.
I'm yours forever, I just wanted you to know.

Time and time again, you were there for me,
Right there by my side,
I thought that I was blinded.
But now I know it wasn't make believe.
Your love has always been so true,
And looking back, I always knew,
Yeah, looking back, my heart belonged to you.

And why did it take me so long
To make your love a song?
And why did it take so long to see
What was right in front of me?
I'm never gonna let you go.
I'm yours forever, I just wanted you to know.

Remember the first time you took my hand?
I think I'll stay here.
I think I'll stay...

And why did it take me so long
To make your love a song?
And why did it take so long to see
What was right in front of me?
I'm never gonna let you go.
I'm yours forever, I just wanted you to know.

I don't realize that I'm openly crying until Sam sets the guitar down and looks at me.

"Oh my - Mel? Are you okay?" He's by my side in an instant, pulling me against his chest. I wrap my arms around him and bury my face into his neck. "The song wasn't that bad, was it?" he jokes, trying to put a smile on my face.

"No. Sam, the song was wonderful," I tell him, wiping my tears away with the tips of my fingers. "It's absolutely my favorite song you've ever written."

"I didn't want it to make you cry," he says.

"No, it didn't. I mean, it did, but only because it's so wonderful. *You're* so wonderful." I know I keep using the same word over and over again, but I'm not feeling my most eloquent. I have a thousand different thoughts and emotions all colliding inside my mind and my heart. Love. Guilt. Exhilaration. Desire. Fear.

"Mel..." He pulls me back against him and presses his lips to my forehead. We sit like that for several moments. Not talking. Not kissing. Just wrapped in each other's warm embrace.

Listening to the strong, steady beat of his heart, I make a decision. I'm going to tell him about Jesse and Tara. I have to. I can't keep something like this from him. It's not fair. He wouldn't keep anything from me. Maybe he'll know what to do. Maybe he'll actually be able to talk some sense into Jesse.

"Hey Sam," I whisper.

"Yeah?" Sam glances down at me.

"I - I have to tell you something."

"Okay." He waits patiently for me to continue.

I take a deep breath, trying to figure out exactly how to begin. I can feel my heart pounding in a totally different way than it usually does when I'm around Sam. Probably because I know I'm about to do a terrible thing. I'm about to reveal a secret that isn't my own. I'm about to betray a friend. But somehow, in keeping that secret, I feel like I'm betraying the person who means the most to me.

"Sam... I..."

But then I look into his eyes, so beautiful and blue and clear. His eyes have always been my favorite of his features. I can always tell exactly what he's thinking. All I have to do

73

is look into his eyes. Right now, I know that it doesn't matter what I say to him. He'll be there for me in any way that he can.

And that's why I can't tell him.

Something like this would shatter him. Sam is the most loyal person I know. With everything he has coming up, I just can't burden him with this. It would be the most selfish thing I've ever done. Sam needs to stay Sam. He needs to believe that his friends are all as caring and loyal and honorable as he is. I want him to believe that. I love him too much to see him hurt.

"What is it, Mel?" he asks softly.

"It's just... you are the best thing that ever happened to me." It's not what I was going to tell him, but it is the truth. No matter what, that is one thing that will always be true.

Sam smiles and kisses me; a long, slow kiss. Then he pulls away, brushes my loose strands of hair away from my face, and whispers, "The feeling is mutual."

CHAPTER 9

"Swim, swim my darlin'
Straight to my shoreline
Let your love flow freely down
You're magical, mystical, ever so ethereal
Take me across your galaxies
Let your smile bring me to my knees
I'm yours, you're mine
My sweet, sweet Pisces..."

Song: "My Pisces"
Artist: Morning Muses
From the Album: *Nightfall*

Last night, I had one of the worst dreams of my life. It wasn't a nightmare, though I have had my share of those in the past. Like the one where I dreamt Josh was a zombie and I had to stab him in the brain. Or the one where I dreamt that I was on a train full of zombies and I couldn't escape. Apparently, all of my nightmares involve zombies. I blame Sam for that.

The dream I had last night was even worse, though. It was a guilt-dream. Ironically, it wasn't about Sam. It wasn't even about Joni or Cory. It was about their mother.

In my dream, we were all back home, hanging out at Sam's house, when all of a sudden, Joni and Cory's mom bursts in and starts screaming my name. I should mention that Mrs. Foreman is one of the sweetest women I know and is kind of like another mom to me. Anyway, in my dream, she was absolutely hysterical. When I asked her what was wrong, she cried, "You knew! You *knew*! My poor baby! My poor Cory! How could you let this happen, Mel? How *could* you?"

Needless to say, I woke up feeling like the scum of the earth.

That does it. I have to talk to Jesse. And it's not because of Joni and it's not because of Cory and it's not even because of Sam. It's because of me. I don't cover up affairs. It's just not who I am. It's not who I want to be. This whole time, I've wanted to do the right thing, but I've never been entirely sure what that was. At first, I thought that keeping quiet and minding my own business was the right thing, but the more I think about it, the more I'm beginning to wonder if by not speaking up, I'm actually silently condoning it. That isn't okay.

The only trick is going to be getting Jesse alone. Unlike Sam, I can't just drag Jesse off for a private conversation and act like it's no big deal. He's my friend, but I've never felt as close to him as I have to the other guys. I'm going to have to be sneaky, clever.

Thankfully, I don't have to wait very long for an opportunity to present itself. The guys are in the middle of their first rehearsal of the year and Cory just called for a five-minute break.

"Good idea, brother. Hey, where's the bathroom?" Jesse asks.

76

A crew member points him down the hall and to the left.

"You know, I could use a restroom break as well," I announce to no one in particular. Nobody is really paying any attention to me. But you know, just covering all my bases and whatnot. I don't want to look suspicious. Granted, it probably doesn't get any more awkward than my little declaration, but oh well. I pulled it off.

I fall back a step or two behind Jesse as I follow him back to the restrooms. We don't talk. He doesn't even acknowledge my presence. He honestly believes I have to go to the bathroom.

Perfect.

Right up until Jesse disappears into his bathroom, I act like I'm about to walk into the girls' room across the hall, but at the last minute, I duck inside the guys' restroom, slam the door shut, and lock it. Jesse whirls around, caught completely off guard.

"Melissa, this is the men's room!" he exclaims. It's kind of funny. He sounds more scandalized than he did when I walked in on him kissing Cory's girlfriend.

"Oh, I know," I assure him. "We need to talk."

"What, now? It can't wait?" Apparently, he had too much orange juice or something this morning because he really seems like he has to go. It's kind of funny to see Jesse Scott acting all human.

"No, because I don't know when else I'll be able to get you alone," I answer.

"Okay, look, you and Sam might have one of those weird relationships where you pee in front of each other, but I just don't think we're that close."

"Noted. And for the record, that has never happened." Sam may be the love of my life, but I think we're both happy to keep some mystery between us, especially when it comes to the toilet. "We need to talk about Tara."

"I thought we already talked about her," he hisses.

77

"We did, but we're going to talk again." This is weird. I'm usually never this assertive. It's unfamiliar, but I kind of like it. I feel so empowered. Granted, I did just corner a guy who was about to unzip his pants before I walked in, but still. "Jesse, I can't do this anymore."

"Can't do what?"

"I can't keep your secret anymore. It's not right. You know it's not right."

"God, I know, I know," Jesse buries his face in his hands. Throughout all of this, I've never thought of Jesse as a bad guy. Just someone with a very limited supply of self-control, especially when it comes to supermodels. "We're still trying to figure everything out."

"You've had over a month to do that. You two either need to come clean, or break it off. And if you don't..."

"What?" he presses.

I take a deep breath and swallow my fear of intimidation and confrontation and just about everything else.

"If you don't, I'm going to tell Cory."

I can tell just by the look on his face that the last thing Jesse wants is to hurt Cory. Jesse isn't one of those sleazy friends in sitcoms who steals girls for the fun of it. He isn't doing this out of any sort of spite or jealousy or contempt. That's what makes this so hard. If he was actually a jerk, I would have no problem threatening to rat him out. But he isn't. He's just misguided and in way over his head. That's no excuse, mind you. But it doesn't make him a bad person. A bad friend, maybe. But not a bad person.

"Why? What is this to you, Mel?"

That throws me off. Jesse never calls me Mel. I'm always Melissa. I guess he's finally being serious with me.

"Because it's eating me up, Jesse. Do you have any idea how much it would hurt Cory if he found out I knew and didn't say anything? Or Joni?"

"They don't have to find out," he tells me.

"But they *will!* It doesn't matter whether they have to or not. Somehow, this is going to get out, and when it does, a lot of hearts are going to be broken. That's why I'm telling you, end this now. Or I will."

Jesse sighs. I think he knows I'm right.

"Okay," he finally murmurs.

"Okay, what?"

"Okay, I'll end it." He sounds sincere, but there is a part of me wondering if he's just saying it to get me out of the bathroom.

"You promise?" I ask, narrowing my eyes.

"I promise. Now, would you maybe, you know, leave?" he asks.

"Oh, right. Of course. Sorry about that."

"Not a problem." That's sarcasm, but I really don't care. As long as he keeps his word and breaks things off with Tara, he can be as snippy and sarcastic as he wants with me.

Feeling like a huge weight has been lifted off my shoulders, I leave the bathroom and head back out to join the rest of the guys in the rehearsal studio. Finally, after all these weeks, I feel like I get to enjoy life again. Finally, I feel like I can breathe.

...

That happy feeling is short-lived. When we break for lunch, I reach into my pocket to check my phone. I'm not sure why. Every person I normally text is sitting in the room with me. Force of habit, I guess.

Anyway, to my surprise, I see that I have a new text message. From Kendra Jackson.

That's strange. Why would she be texting me? I mean, yeah, we reconnected at my birthday party, and I did have to apologize for that whole mess with people thinking that she's the one dating Sam, but neither of us are big texters. Something has to be wrong.

And it is.

Don't panic, but I think I have a stalker.

"*What?!*" The yelp is out of my mouth before I can stop it.

"Mel?" Sam glances over at me. "Everything okay?"

I don't know how to answer him. I am totally freaking out. *Don't panic?* How is this a *don't panic* situation?

"Not really," I answer.

"What's going on?" Joni asks.

Six pairs of curious eyes are now on me. Actually, make that eight. Neil and Chris from the band are eavesdropping too. This is too much.

"Uh... I'll be right back. I need to go make a phone call." And without another word, I leap up and sprint into the hallway. With trembling fingers, I hit the **Call** button next to Kendra's name. While I wait for her to answer, Sam jogs into the hall, his handsome face lined with concern.

Are you okay? he mouths.

I nod in response as Kendra answers.

"Hello?"

"Kendra! It's Mel." I don't know why I need to tell her that. I'm assuming she figured out it was me when she saw my name pop up on her smartphone screen. She is a genius, after all.

"Hey. You're panicking, aren't you?" she asks.

"*Yes*, I'm panicking. Any normal person would panic when their friend tells them that she has a stalker!"

"*What?*" Sam exclaims. See, we even react to crises the same way. This is why we're so obviously meant to be. But now's not the time for starry-eyed romance. I hold up my hand to silence him.

"I don't think she's *that* kind of stalker. I don't think she wants to hurt me," Kendra assures me. "I think she's an obsessive The Kind of September fan."

"Do you know her name?"

"I think it's something like Alicia Thompson."

Oh my *God*! I actually know who that girl is! We had a real problem with her last year. Somehow, she managed to

80

track down a few of the guys' extended family members and began writing them really long and detailed messages about why they should give her the guys' phone numbers and private email addresses. The best was when she sent Josh's cousin an extensive list of all the reasons she deserved to meet the guys. One of them was, and I quote, "*Because I'm not a crazy, obsessive stalker.*"

Thankfully, this girl has never actually appeared to anyone in person. It's all been online interaction. Still, it can be unnerving, especially for someone like Kendra who isn't used to the limelight at all. Heck, *I'm* not used to the limelight and I work in tangent to it!

"Oh, Kendra, I am so sorry," I tell her and briefly explain to her that this isn't the first time Alicia has overstepped her boundaries.

"It's not your fault, Mel. Besides, I'm not too concerned about me. It's my family. Apparently she's been sending creepy emails to my mother full of inappropriate questions about Sam and me."

Okay, that *is* really creepy.

"Tell your mother not to respond. Do not engage this girl in any way," I tell her.

"Oh, don't worry. She blocked her. But then a few days later, she tracked down my older brother and tried to persuade him to give her my phone number. I'm telling you Mel, I don't know how you put up with this on a daily basis."

"Well, I don't, really," I say. Though, that will probably change whenever Sam and I decided to go public with our relationship. "The guys though have just had to learn to love and embrace the true fans and to ignore the creepers."

"That's what I'm trying to do. It's just frustrating that she's bringing my family into this. Not to mention the fact that it turns out there are more The Kind of September fans at CalTech than I thought. I've had more than a dozen people

81

approach me and ask if it's true that I'm dating Sam. I even caught one of them trying to take my picture."

"Oh, God. I'm sorry," I apologize again. I know she'll say that it's not my fault, but I still feel responsible for inviting her to my birthday party. "If you want, I'll tell Sam to say something on Twitter."

"No, I think it will all die down soon enough. I am glad to know that you think Alicia is harmless, though."

"Yeah, I don't think you have to worry. She's crazy and she's really creepy, but she's not dangerous," I assure her.

"Are you talking about that Alicia girl?" Sam hisses. I nod. "Tell Kendra to just ignore her. And that I'll say something about being single on Twitter tonight."

I repeat his sentiments and Kendra expresses her gratitude. We chat for another minute or so before she has to be on her way to work. Sam and I probably need to head back as well. Lunch is almost over and I know the others are wondering just what the heck is going on.

After Kendra and I hang up, I turn to face Sam. He looks a bit frazzled, but thankfully, he's got his wits about him.

"You know, one of these days, I'm going to do something so extravagant and scandalous that no one is going to care about who I date." He's trying to keep the mood light, but I can tell he's frustrated. I don't blame him. As far as Sam is concerned, no woman is safe as long as they're associated with him. And I guess Alicia Thompson and the tabloids are kind of proving him right.

"Like what?" I ask, going along with it.

"Like paint myself red and run naked down Santa Monica Boulevard."

"Yeah, that would do it."

"Would you still want to go out with me?"

"Probably. But you'd never actually get me to admit that we were dating."

"That might be in your best interests," he mutters, uncharacteristically down on himself.

"Hey." I take both his hands in mine. "We've talked about this. Everything is going to be fine. No matter what happens, we'll get through it together. Okay?"

He smiles down at me.

"No wonder I love you so much."

Then he steals a quick kiss before we both head back out to face the literal and metaphorical music.

CHAPTER 10

"Boats coming in
Crossing the seas
Winds that are forever
Chasing me
Still when the world turns
And fades into gray
I'll stand on the shoreline
Till that fateful day
And there on Iona I'll wait..."

Song: "Iona"
Artist: The Kind of September
From the Album: *Meet Me on the Midway* (Bonus
Track)

The guys have a well-deserved day off tomorrow, so
Sam has declared tonight our first official date night on the
road. Of course, technically we're not really on the road yet,
but who cares? I get to spend a romantic evening in a fancy
hotel with the man that I love.

Luckily, Joni informed me earlier that she's going to be
out late in a meeting with Stan, the guys' stage manager, and

the rest of the crew. I asked her if she needed me to be there too, but she told me they were just going over a bunch of formalities and that if they said anything that I absolutely needed to hear, she would write it down and pass it on. Let me tell you, that is fine by me. I've been to a few of those meetings before. They can get a little tedious.

So since Joni will be out for a few hours, I offered to host date night in our room. Let's face it, even though house-keeping cleans Sam and Cory's room every day, there's always a chance something might come crawling out of one of their suitcases. But because Sam and I will be in our room, I made a point to ask Joni to text me when she was on her way back. Even though she'll probably be the first one I tell about Sam and me, I'm definitely not ready yet, and I don't think Joni is ready to hear it yet, either. There's simply too much going on right now.

Besides, I kind of want to enjoy our secret just a little while longer.

Most of our date nights so far have been pretty casual. We'll order a pizza and watch a movie in our pajamas. And I love those date nights. They remind me of all the reasons I fell in love with Sam in the first place. The *real* Sam. The Sam who likes to pretend he's training for the zombie apocalypse while he's at the gym, and who not-so-secretly likes to sing Ed Sheeran songs at the top of his lungs while he's in the shower. The Sam who isn't an international superstar.

But since tonight is our first date night "on the road," I want to make it special. I thought about trying to cook something, but then I remembered that the only thing I know how to make is spaghetti and that Sam is the only person I know who eats spaghetti without the sauce. I'm serious. He eats the pasta plain with butter and a sprinkle of Parmesan cheese. He's never come out and said it, but I think he eats it that way because it reminds him of the way his dad used to make it for him.

85

Sam's dad, Thomas, died when we were only six. That's why Sam and his family moved to the Bay Area, to be close to Thomas' parents while he underwent chemo and radiation. I don't remember his dad very well, only that he was already sick when Sam and I met. The day after Thomas died, I sat with Sam on the front porch of their tiny apartment for hours. We didn't talk about a whole lot. We just watched the cars passing by. It might sound crazy, or even a little insensitive, but I think that was the day I realized that I would never meet another boy who mattered to me more than Sam. And I haven't.

Which brings me back to why I decided not to cook tonight. I want this first date to be amazing and wonderful and everything that Sam deserves, and it just won't be if I try to cook. In fact, it would be a disaster. I might even accidentally burn down the hotel. One day, I would love to learn to cook, but I'm afraid it's just not going to happen in a few short hours.

Before he arrives, I shower and style my hair, pulling half of it up into a ponytail and letting the rest fall in light brown waves down past my shoulders. Then I brush my teeth and apply a bit of mascara, eye shadow, and lip gloss. I know I don't need to wear makeup to impress Sam, but some nights, I like to look pretty just for me. Tonight is one of those nights. For my outfit, I select a short-sleeved, peach-colored dress and a brown belt. I add a gold necklace and gold earrings for a touch of accent. Finally, I spritz on a bit of my favorite perfume and slip on my pair of brown ankle boots that my sister got me for Christmas. I try, but Brooklyn is the true fashionista of the family. Still, I think I look pretty cute tonight.

I take the last few minutes before Sam arrives to run around the room, making sure everything is neat and tidy. I don't know why, but I'm a little nervous. It's not that this is our actual first date, but it does kind of feel like the first time we'll be really, really alone. No parents, no siblings, no bandmates. Sam told them that he was going to give them an excuse, but as long as the rest of them have a place to hang out and eat junk food, they don't care what he does.

I'm double checking my reflection in the mirror when someone knocks on the door. I'm half-expecting him to jokingly call out, "Housekeeping!" But he remains silent.

My heart skips at least five beats when I open the door and see him standing there, looking unbearably handsome in sleek black slacks, a white button-down shirt, and a new black jacket that I've never seen before. I must have a stunned expression or something on my face because Sam laughs and asks, "Too much?"

"No," I breathe. "You look... I mean... Oh, wow..."

"You don't look too bad yourself, Lovely. Is that a new dress?"

"Yeah," I answer automatically. It's actually not a new dress. I got it last spring and then forgot about it. So I guess it is kind of new.

"It is very becoming," Sam tells me, placing his hands on my hips and pulling me into a kiss. I've just wrapped my arms around his neck when another door opens somewhere down the hall. Sam glances around, then turns back to me. "We should probably close the door."

"Good idea," I agree.

Once we're alone inside, Sam picks up right where we left off, brushing a few loose strands of hair away from my face and kissing me. Usually, our evenings start off slowly, with a bit of casual small talk or playful flirtation. Not tonight. Tonight is white, blinding ecstasy. I'm so lost in his touch and his embrace that I don't realize we've been moving until my legs hit the side of my bed. It's only then that Sam pulls his lips away from mine.

"Hi," he murmurs, sounding as breathless as I feel.

"Hi," I whisper back.

We stand there a few moments longer, in a beautiful and passionate silence, simply savoring each other's presence.

I listen to the sound of him breathing and smile as his messy locks of dark blond hair tickle the bridge of my nose.

"Do you know how much I've missed being alone with you?" Sam asks.

I do. It's been nearly two weeks since the night he played me the song that he wrote and even though we've seen each other every day since, it's just not the same.

"I think I might have an idea."

Sam responds by closing his eyes and kissing me again. I wish I knew exactly what he was thinking. When he's near me, my entire world spirals into a frenzy. Suddenly, my blood is pulsing with electricity and my mind is spinning in a whirlwind of pleasure and love and a million other things. Sam, on the other hand, seems totally at ease. It's almost like my touch has a soothing effect on him. Not in a bad way. He's just so confident and expressive and always seems to know exactly what he's doing. I've always envied him that.

Before I know what's happening, he breaks away from my mouth and his lips travel along my jawline to my neck. *This* has never happened before. Without really thinking, I close my eyes again and lean into him, nuzzling my face into his neck.

And then, without warning, he breaks away.

"What's the matter?" I wonder.

"Nothing, nothing. I just think I might be getting a little carried away," he admits sheepishly. "I don't want to make you feel pressured."

"You're not," I assure him.

"I know. But I'm afraid that if we keep it up, then I will."

Sam and I have already had this talk once before. It was our first week home over break. Long story short, he's a bit more experienced than I am when it comes to relationships. In the back of my mind, I kind of always knew it, but having him confirm it... well, it made me a little anxious. Let's face it, the closest I've gotten to sex is the car

88

scene from *Titanic*. And I wasn't even allowed to see that until I was sixteen.

Anyway, Sam could tell that the subject made me a little apprehensive. I don't want it to. I love him and I want to be with him. But I also want it to be a good experience for both of us. I want to be ready for it. And right now... I'm just not sure that I am.

Sam understands, and thank goodness he does. You meet a lot of great guys in the music industry, but you also meet a lot of scum bags who have absolutely no respect for women. Actually, I think that's probably any industry, but this is the only one I know.

"I love you," I tell Sam.

"I love you, too." He kisses me swiftly on the forehead. "So... What are you thinking for dinner?"

We end up ordering in from a local cafe. Sam gets a turkey and ham club sandwich with chips and I decide on a bread bowl of cheddar broccoli soup. To top it all off, we each order a slice of cheesecake. It might be the most amazing meal I've ever had. Much better than it would have been if I had ended up trying to cook.

"So, have you heard from Kendra lately?" Sam asks, shoveling his last bite of cheesecake into his mouth.

"Yeah, I texted her a few days ago. Things are finally calming down for her."

"That's good. I told the guys what had been going on and Cory was asking me about her this afternoon. I think they were all a little rattled when they heard Alicia was back. Speaking of, I think we need a strategy."

"What do you mean?"

"I mean, eventually someone is going to see the two of us spending time together alone. Or a stray paparazzi is going to snap a picture of us looking like more-than-friends and what happened to Kendra is going to happen to you."

"It's kind of already has happened to me. Remember Meliver? I came through that unscathed. Besides, everyone already knows that you and I are friends. I've been associated with you for years now. Face it, Sam, I'm kind of old news."

"You'll never be old news, Mel," he tells me.

"You're biased."

"Maybe a little. Still, better safe than sorry."

"Well, look, when the time comes that we decide to tell people, let's do it the right way. Let's just be honest. I think that will be a lot better than getting caught sneaking out of a hotel room or having somebody else out us. But until we're ready, we can just tell people that I've been promoted to your assistant."

"Are you kidding?" Sam laughs.

"What? Couldn't you use an assistant?"

"Yeah, but doesn't that sound a little degrading? You're my best friend. You're my girlfriend!"

"Okay then, we say that we're best friends and have been for years. Most of the fans already know that." I scoot my chair closer to his and take his hand.

"I guess I'm just being a little paranoid. First with the whole Chloe Conley debacle, then Alicia resurfacing..."

"You don't have to explain, Sam. I know you want to protect me. And I love you for that. But remember, I've been with you since the beginning. I've seen everything that's gone down whenever a new girl comes into your life. I know what I'm getting myself into, but I don't care, because I get you."

"Well, between you and me, I think I got the better end of the deal," he smiles, running his fingertips along the palm of my hand. Now how does he expect me to think clearly when he's looking at me like that?

"I don't think so," I laugh, blushing furiously.

"It's definitely true. For as long as I've known you, you've always underestimated your value. But you're kind, you're warm, you're loyal... You are the most genuine person I've ever known. And you're beautiful. You'll never admit it, but you are. Inside and out. And I'll always love you for it."

90

"Oh, Sam..." Why does he always have to make me cry when we're alone? I don't have words like that to express how he makes me feel. I wish I did. But I'm only equipped with the simplest form of expression: an embrace, a kiss, and the words, "I love you."

And I hope, more than anything, that that's enough.

CHAPTER 11

"Light up my life
With those blue eyes
Oh girl, you've got me
Hypnotized
You're Heaven sent
Bet you could fly
Just beyond these indigo skies..."

Song: "Indigo"
Artist: The Kind of September
From the Album: *The Kind of September*

Today is going to be stressful for a few reasons.

For one thing, my online classes start up again, and this semester, I'm taking a Statistics and Data class that I can already tell is going to ruin my life. I glanced over the syllabus last night and within two minutes, I was ready to cry. I was never any good at math in high school and now I'll be studying what looks to be some sort of alien language on my own. I'm hoping that Joni might be able to help me, but she's been awfully distracted lately. I was already asleep by the time she came back from her meeting the other night. When I asked her about it in the morning, she said it had gone well, but that her work load was going to be increasing. I'm halfway hoping Stan and the managers will give me more to do so after I fail out of Statistic, I'll have a legitimate excuse to give my parents.

For another thing, the guys have already started working on songs for the next album and have decided that they want to incorporate a few new numbers into their set list. The songs are great and I know the fans will be thrilled, but it's thrown a bit of a curve ball into the rehearsal schedule. Not to mention the extra choreography sessions and the extra song-writing sessions, which is what's going on right now.

And the third reason today is going to be stressful? Tara just walked in. And I'm the only one in sight.

My first instinct when I saw those white designer sunglasses and flowing locks of blonde hair was to run and hide, but I figure that might look a bit suspicious. For all I know, Jesse didn't even mention my name when he broke things off with her. He could have told her that he knew in his heart it was wrong to betray his friend and that as much as he liked her and found her attractive, he simply couldn't see her anymore.

"Melissa," she greets me with an icy sneer.

Or he could have thrown me under the bus like yesterday's lunch.

"Hey, Tara. It is good to see you again. I hate to run off, but I have a lot of work to get done before -"

"Oh, I think you can take a moment or two." Her tone is threateningly sweet; nice enough so as not to alert anyone who might happen to overhear her, but menacing enough to let me know that I am, in fact, about to die.

"Um. Okay. Well, why don't I just let Joni know -"

"No one will miss you. Come on." And with that, she practically drags me off to one of the storage closets in the back of the studio. She slams the door shut, flips on the light switch, and stares me down with her hands on her hips. You wouldn't believe how much more intimidating a supermodel can look under fluorescent lights. "Exactly *who* do you think you are?"

"Well, I -"

"You *threatened* him?! And after all that we've been through together? After all we've done for you?" she demands.

"I'm sorry. What have you done for me, exactly?" I ask.

"Look around you! Do you think you'd be here today without Jesse?" As I glance around the storage closet full of fold-up chairs, old microphones, and cleaning supplies, I can't help but hope that she sees the irony in what she's asking me.

"No, I know I wouldn't be here if it weren't for him," I remark.

"Then why couldn't you do this one thing for him? Do you have any idea how happy he was with me?"

"Do you have any idea how happy Cory is with you?" I counter. "Tara, that boy is crazy about you. He worships the ground you walk on. If you want to date Jesse, fine, but at least have the decency to be honest with Cory."

"Oh, Melissa, you are so out of your depth here. Let me guess. You've never even kissed a guy, have you?"

"What is *that* supposed to mean?"

"It means that you have no idea what it means to be in a real relationship."

By this point, I'm so angry that I'm beginning to feel light-headed. Just what is she trying to insinuate here? That I'm naive because I think that it's wrong for her to be cheating on my friend?

"Listen Tara, I might not be hooking up with two guys at once, but I do know a thing or two about what it means to care about someone. And from where I'm standing, it doesn't

94

seem like you care about Cory *or* Jesse. In fact, if you ask me, dumping you was the smartest thing Jesse ever did."

Big. Mistake.

The next thing I know, Tara's hands are on my shoulders. Suddenly, I'm flying backwards into the stacks of chairs and dusty amplifiers. I land with a loud THUD, sending chairs, boxes, and even a table crashing to the ground. Thankfully, I don't think anything in here is irreplaceable or even that valuable.

Tara, meanwhile, glares down at me, her eyes narrow, her scowl fierce.

"You mess with me or Jesse again, and I *will* expose you for the rat-faced little backstabber that you are. You got that?"

I'm a little afraid that if I actually say anything I'll start to whimper. Now that I'm over the initial shock of being shoved to the ground, I'm beginning to feel bruises blossoming across my back and down my arms. So I simply nod.

"Good," Tara spits. Then she turns on her heel and marches back out into the studio.

...

After cleaning up the mess in the storage closet, I sneak off to the backstage bathroom where the guys keep their first aid kit. You'd be surprised just how many injuries are sustained when we're on the road. Of all the guys, I'd say Josh is injured the most, just because he's the most energetic and likes to run around and play sports and perform the occasional strip-tease on a collapsible table.

Oliver, on the other hand, is the klutziest. He doesn't try to hurt himself. It just kind of happens. He's cut himself with scissors, burned himself with a hot blow dryer, broken his toe running out on stage... The poor boy is just a mess.

Then you have Sam and Jesse who like to rough-house. They'll get into these stupid fake wrestling matches and more often than not, they'll drag the rest of the guys into it as well, resulting in bruises and scratch marks. I don't know why they do this, but every single time, they remind me of puppies who think they're a lot tougher and scarier than they actually are.

Cory is the only one of the guys who rarely needs medical attention. Though he did get a splinter last year and he made a big deal out of it for like a week.

As for me, I'm a bit more beat up than I thought. I have several scrapes and cuts down my arms, a few of which have been bleeding. I apparently also hit the side of my face because I've got a scrape across the side of my forehead. Thankfully, that one is only a superficial wound and didn't bleed very much. As for the bruises, they're all still rather fresh, but I imagine that by tomorrow, my shoulders and back will just be covered in purple and green splotches. Gross.

Once I've tended to my open wounds, I try to come up with a plausible explanation behind my new zombie look. It's not like my friends won't notice that I'm suddenly sporting a large red mark on my face or three new band aids down my arms.

Sure enough, the moment I leave the backstage area, Joni comes flying toward me.

"Where have you been? I've been looking for you everywhere. The guys are doing that thing where they want - what happened?!" she gasps.

"Oh, my face?" I ask, trying to play it like it's not a big deal and I already forgot about it.

"And your arms. And your shirt. You've got a huge rip in your sleeve."

"Huh. Didn't notice that," I mutter, glancing over my shoulder.

"Mel, what happened to you? Are you okay?"

"Oh yeah, I'm fine. Just had a bit of a tumble, that's all."

"What were you doing?"

"I was looking for something in the supply closet and... I thought I saw a bug." Excellent. That totally sounds like me. I'm terrified of bugs. I mean honestly, who isn't? "I lost my balance and fell straight into those stacks of chairs."

"Well, I hope that if there actually was a bug, you crushed it," Joni remarks.

"Yeah, me too." Although I know for a fact that that's not the case. If anything, I'm the one who's going to end up crushed. "Anyway, what were you going to say?"

"Oh, Sam sent me to find you. They've finished writing their new song and they're refusing to perform it until everyone is present and accounted for. Of course, that also means the wicked witch of Hollywood Boulevard will be there too." Joni rolls her eyes.

"Great," I mutter.

"Well, at least she's nice to you."

"Yeah. Not anymore," I scoff.

"How come?"

Oops.

That was a stupid slip. It was bad enough when Tara was being nice to me and I claimed not to know why. But now that she's reverted back to her evil ways, Joni is going to begin to wonder if something hasn't been going on that I haven't told her about. And there totally has.

"Who knows? I probably insulted her with my face or something."

And what do you know? Joni actually accepts that as a plausible explanation. Tara annoys her that much.

"God, she's the worst. You know, I really thought that my brother would be over her by now."

"I think we were all kind of hoping that, but here we are," I sigh. "I guess you can't help who you fall in love with."

"I guess," Joni agrees. That's oddly sentimental for her. "But why did it have to be someone so awful? Doesn't he realize he could have anyone? Someone smart and funny and actually a decent person? Of course not. Because he's an idiot." Okay, that's more like the Joni I know and love. I was afraid I'd lost her there for a second.

97

Tara is already there and hanging all over Cory when Joni and I walk into the room where the guys have been writing and rehearsing. It kind of looks like a conference room, with four tables arranged into a square and a dozen chairs situated all around the floor. There's even a counter, complete with sink, cabinets, and a coffee-maker.

Sam, Oliver, and Josh are all sitting at the tables, surrounded by dozens of sheets of notes, lyrics, and music, while Jesse paces around, strumming his guitar. I can't help but notice he's refusing to look at Tara, who's currently twirling one of Cory's curls around her perfectly manicured finger.

"Alright, we're here," Joni announces.

Sam glances up, a huge grin on his face, but it fades immediately when he looks at me. Just like that, he's up, out of his chair, and crossing the room.

"Mel, oh my God. What happened?" he asks, inspecting the scrape across my forehead.

"Nothing. Just tripped," I assure him.

"She saw a bug," Joni quips.

"Yeah, that too." I forgot that I'd made that up. Thankfully Joni's always there to keep my stories straight, even when they're not true.

"Are you sure you're okay? That looks serious. You might have a concussion," Sam says.

"It looks a lot worse than it is." By now, everyone in the room, including Cory and Tara, are staring at me. I make a point to avoid eye contact with both of them.

Please, make it stop. Please, make it stop.

"Well, still, maybe you should take it easy for the rest of the day," Sam suggests. Have I mentioned how much I love that he's so protective of me?

"Deal. But first I want to hear this new song." And *that* is how you draw the attention away from yourself in a room full of musicians.

"Right!" Sam claps his hands together. "Well, this isn't really an idea we've had for very long. It just kind of came to Josh the other night."

"I wanted to write a name song, you know? Like I'm talking to a girl. I feel like all the greats have at least one song that's a name," Josh explains. "Well, you'll hear it. Take it away, Mr. Scott."

"One, two... One, two, three..." Jesse strikes up a few fast, upbeat chords and the song begins.

Oliver:
See that girl
Singing to herself
In a red dress
So beautiful, beautiful.

Cory:
All the people
That pass her by
Can't help but stare
She's got that light.

Sam:
All this time,
I can't help thinking
Oh this girl,
She could really shine.

All:
And I say, hey Daphne,
What do you say?
Do you want to be a star someday?
With your name in shining lights,
You know, this feels so right, girl.
Hey, Daphne,
Look at you now,

99

Just take a breath and show them how.
Nothing's gonna stand in your way.
What do you say, girl?

Jesse:
Now she's here
Dancing in my arms
In a red dress
So beautiful, beautiful.

Josh:
Like a fairy tale
Once upon a time
I can't help but stare
She's got that light.

Sam:
All this time,
I can't help thinking
There must be some way
To make her mine.

All:
And I say, hey Daphne,
What do you say?
Do you want to be a star someday?
With your name in shining lights,
You know, this feels so right, girl.
Hey, Daphne,
Look at you now,
Just take a breath and show them how.
Nothing's gonna stand in your way.
What do you say, girl?

Sam:
And I don't know
How this story ends

But I hope
You make it worth your while...

All:
And I say, hey Daphne,
What do you say?
Told you that we'd reach the stars someday.
With our names in shining lights,
You know, this feels so right, girl.
Hey, Daphne,
Look at us now,
We'll take a breath and show them how.
Nothing's gonna stand in our way.
What do you say, girl?
Yeah, just what do you say, girl?
What do you say?

Once the song ends, Josh flashes us one of his supersonic grins and asks, "So... what do you think?"

I don't know how to break it to Josh without inflating his already exceptionally large ego, but I think this might be one of the best songs that they've ever written. It's catchy, it's fun, and it's different, but in a good way. I think this could definitely be their next single.

"It's excellent, Josh," I tell him. "I loved it."

"Aw. Thank you, Mel."

"I agree. Good job, guys," Joni, never one to gush, says.

"Who's Daphne?" Tara asks.

"I don't know. Just liked the name," Josh shrugs.

"What did you think of the song, Babe?" Cory asks his girlfriend.

"I mean, it was okay. But I like your older stuff better." Tara crosses her arms, a bit of a pout on her shiny, pink lips.

"In other words, job well done, lads," Oliver remarks.

I have to fight back a laugh. I'm just stunned that Oliver -

101

sweet, sweatered, oh so British *Oliver* - would say such a thing! Joni, on the other hand, isn't even trying to hide her amusement.

"Oliver, you just made my whole day," Joni snickers. Oliver blushes, a goofy grin on his face. Joni has no idea, but she just made his day as well.

Maybe I should mention something to her...

No! I'm already involved in too many peoples' relationships as it is! So many that I barely have time to enjoy my own romance! It's settled. No matter how cute I think Joni and Oliver would be together, I've got to start minding my own business. Their lives are theirs. Not mine. I do not know what's best for them or anyone else.

At least, that's what I'm going to keep telling myself.

CHAPTER 12

"On the brink of a summer day
You began to look my way
I fell and oh, I never looked back
Humid nights, on the Fourth of July
Your name was painted in the sky
Fireworks against the black..."

Song: "Independence"
Artist: Chloe Conley
From the Album: *Chloe*

It's the first weekend in February and the guys have been invited to attend the opening of a new nightclub in LA tonight. It's called Club Asteria and it's supposed to be really cool... and *very* exclusive. It's basically impossible to get in unless you're on the proverbial List or you know someone on said List.

This isn't the first time the guys have been asked to attend the opening of a trendy new club. It is the first time, however, that I'll be going with them. I think they were all surprised that I said yes after Sam invited me. After all, they've invited me before and I've always come up with an excuse not to go. It wasn't that I didn't want to hang out with them. It's just that night clubs have never really been my scene. But now that I'm with Sam, I kind of want to experience one.

That, and he told me that he really, really wants me to go. Honestly, with those big blue eyes and that adorable grin, how am I supposed to say no?

So, that's what Joni and I are doing now. Getting all dressed up to go to a fancy celebrity nightclub. Joni has been to a few of these before so she's giving me a few guidelines on how to act.

"First of all, there are going to be photographers and lots of reporters there. You've seen it all before, but you're actually going to be a part of it tonight. That means acting natural. Pretend all the people with microphones and cameras don't even exists," she advises.

"I think I can do that," I say.

"Good. Secondly, no matter what, don't do that thing where you go all starry-eyed when you see someone famous."

"What? I don't do that."

"What's the name of that Irish guitar player you all but proposed to last summer?"

"Okay, I did not propose to him. I simply told him that I enjoy his music." I may have also cyber-stalked him a bit. But that was before I knew that Sam felt the same way about me as I did about him. So you see, I don't need my handsome Irish backup plan anymore.

"All I'm saying is if you're going to fit in in this crowd, you're going to have to act like you belong there. That means playing it cool."

"Fine, I get it. No fangirling."

"And last but not least, you've got to be aware of your surroundings," Joni tells me. "This opening tonight is going to be huge. There will be people everywhere, drinks will be flowing, you could easily get separated or overwhelmed or attract unwanted attention."

"No offense Jo, but you do remember I'm twenty-one, right? I can take care of myself."

"I know, but come on, Mel. I know you. You're not exactly a seasoned party-goer. I just want to make sure you know what you're getting into and that you're prepared. That's all."

"And I appreciate it. Thanks." It's true. I do appreciate Joni looking out for me. I know that I'm not the most street-smart girl in the world. In fact, my experience in most areas is excruciatingly limited. But I think I'll be okay tonight. Especially if Sam is there.

Thanks to Joni (and a few make-up tutorials on YouTube), I at least look like I belong at a super-hip Hollywood nightclub. My hair is styled up in a loose, elegant bun and I've actually taken the time to contour my face, making me look much older than I really am. For just a touch of color, I've shaded my light brown eyes with dark blue eyeshadow. To complete the Cool Party Girl look, I've selected my little black dress and strappy black heels. I'm not very used to the shoes, however, so I'll have to be extra careful, especially if there's any dancing tonight.

When Joni and I meet the guys in the hotel hallway to head out to the limo, Josh lets out a loud wolf-whistle.

"Ow, ladies. Look at you two! Well done, well done. And just so you know, you don't have to worry about fighting over me. There's plenty of Josh to go around," he assures us.

"Oh, that's good to know. I didn't want to have to roundhouse kick Mel in these heels," Joni deadpans. She looks absolutely gorgeous in a form-fitting teal and gold dress with gold shoes to match. For the evening, she straightened her hair, which makes her even more beautiful.

"I guess you ladies don't look too shabby," Jesse comments. "I *might* consider being seen with you."

Sam, meanwhile, simply stares at me with a sort of star struck look in his eyes.

"Wow," he breathes. He's looking pretty good himself in black skinny jeans, a white button-down shirt, and charcoal gray blazer. Then again, does he ever *not* look good?

"What is this? The great Sam Morneau speechless?" Cory laughs. "Maybe you girls should dress up more often."

"That is a spectacular idea," Oliver exclaims. I can't help but notice he is suddenly very red around the ears.

"Alright, alright, they look hot, we look hot, we're all exceptionally attractive people. Now let's get out of this hotel and down to Hollywood. It's time to par-tay!" Josh whoops. Then he holds out both of his elbows to Joni and me. "Ladies? Allow me to be your escort?" I laugh and take his arm. Joni rolls her eyes, but she smiles nevertheless and links her arm through his as well. "Alright! The Josh-Meister is in the house! Or he's about to be!"

Still giggling, I turn around and flash a quick, flirtatious grin towards Sam, who scowls playfully in return. Of course, he knows this is all in good fun. I'd never intentionally try to make him jealous.

And if I were to try, it would probably be with someone other than Josh. Probably a drummer. Because you know, apparently, I have a thing for them.

...

Even though Club Asteria is just a few blocks away, it takes us nearly forty-five minutes to arrive at its front doors. I used to think San Francisco traffic was bad. It's nothing compared to the nightmare that is Los Angeles traffic. Sometimes I wonder if I really am a city girl at heart. I love the lights, I love the culture, and I love the electricity that seems to bring each and every city to life in its own unique way. But as I've gotten older, I've come to find I also love the quiet. I love the tranquility of forests and the soothing lull of lazy waves lapping the coast of a small beach town. This might sound strange, but there are times that I like being alone.

Of course, judging from the looks of Club Asteria, I don't think solitude is going to be an option tonight.

Traffic is bumper-to-bumper outside the nightclub, with several white and black limousines lining both sides of the street and stretching around the block. A sea of reporters, photographers, and onlookers hoping to get in crowd the sidewalk outside the club's entrance. Searchlights dance from the roof of the building, illuminating the already vibrant night sky, and even from the curb, I can see an erratic stream of lights, blue and purple and red and green, pulsating from inside the club. I don't know why, but I feel like I'm about to enter another dimension. Or maybe an alien spaceship.

Sam catches me staring at the scene just outside our limousine window and nudges me with his shoulder.

"You ready for this?" he asks me.

"I think so...?" I'm so nervous, I answer in the form of a question.

"You'll be just fine," he promises. Then he opens the door.

The crowd goes absolutely nuts. Screams erupt from all around. Camera flashes from every angle disrupt and distort my vision. I try to tell myself it's no different than being at a concert, or another one of the guys' events.

But there is a difference. I can't hide behind my camera here. Tonight, I'm a guest. I'm almost a celebrity, or at least a VIP. It's strange and it's terrifying, but I somehow manage to hold my head high, and I think I even smile a little.

The guys take a few moments to talk to fans and reporters outside before we finally make our way inside the club. It turns out I wasn't too far off with the whole alien spacecraft analogy. The walls themselves are painted black and shimmering with hundreds - no, thousands - of lights that look like stars, though it's difficult to see the details through the throngs of people inside. In fact, it's difficult to see much of anything. For a place with so many different colored lights, it's awfully dark inside Club Asteria. Perhaps that's just a characteristic of clubs in general.

It's also *loud*. The techno dance music, full of fast beats and melodies that don't quite make sense, is something of an assault on my eardrums. Granted, I've attended every single concert the guys have ever performed, so I'm used to music so loud that I can feel the bass and drums pounding in your chest, but at least that's music I enjoy. And I usually have some sort of headset to protect my ears. This place, with its deafening stereo system and hypnotic lighting, seems like it was designed to help people lose themselves.

"How great is this?!" Josh exclaims. He has to yell to be heard above all the noise.

"Incredible!" Cory agrees. "I wish Tara was here. She would just love this!"

"Oh, yeah. This is definitely her crowd," Joni remarks. "I bet all the publicity she's missing out on is just killing her."

I know she's probably right, but I'm willing to bet that Tara isn't *too* heartbroken about not being here tonight. She's currently modeling bikinis on the sandy shores of Hawaii. If she does start to feel sad about not being here, she can just order a rum drink in a coconut and lounge on the beach for a few hours. That would make *me* happy.

Actually, I've never tried rum, but I hear daiquiris are really good. Maybe I'll order one tonight. I am twenty-one now, after all. I should enjoy this. But first, I have to figure out where I'm going and do my best not to get separated from the group.

As it turns out, that's easier said than done in a night club packed to the brim with people dancing and drinking and vying for their favorite celebrities' attention. Before I really know what's happening, I'm surrounded by a crowd of strangers and my head is spinning from all the hustle and bustle going on around me.

Somehow, I manage to make it to the bar. The entire counter glows an electric blue and the shelves of liquor bottles behind the bar are all lit up in an array of whites and purples. It's actually sort of pretty.

"What can I get you?" the female bar tender calls out to me.

I think about ordering my rum drink, but I'm so overwhelmed that I don't think alcohol would be a very good idea.

"Can I just get a Coke?" I ask.

"Coming right up."

While I wait for my drink, I look around the room for any sign of my friends. I wonder if they've even noticed that I'm not with them. I like to think they have, Sam especially. But it's so busy and crowded in here, they might be lost themselves.

Just as I'm getting ready to pull out my phone and text Sam and Joni, a pretty, petite girl with wavy strawberry blonde hair takes a seat next to me. I know her face but we've never been properly introduced.

International Pop Princess, Chloe Conley.

I don't know if I should say hello to her or if I should try to sneak off before she notices me. I'm not sure she would recognize me or not, but if she did, things could get very awkward very quickly. It was only a few months ago that rumors circulated that she and Sam were an item, a rumor somewhat ignited by Sam himself. The year before that, the same gossip spread about her and Josh. Josh can't stand her, but Sam seems to think she's pretty okay. I don't know her well enough to have formed a real opinion of her, but I do like her music.

Before I can get up and move, however, she glances over in my direction and asks, "Could this music be any louder?"

"Maybe if they wanted to break the sound barrier," I reply with a laugh. Chloe grins too.

109

"I'm guessing this is what people hear at concerts, but wow. I just can't get used to it."

"I'm with you on that one. That, and it's way too crowded in here."

"Oh my God, right?" she asks. "You look familiar. Have we met?"

"Maybe briefly? I'm Mel Parker."

"Oh, right! You're Sam's friend, right? From the Kind of September?"

"That's me," I grin. "And I, of course, know who you are. I love your music."

"Aw, thank you. That's so sweet. And it's nice to officially meet you."

"You too."

"So, did the guys drag you out here?" Chloe asks.

"Yeah. I wasn't really sure what to expect. I just wanted to come out and support them."

"That's nice of you. I wish I didn't have to be here," she admits.

"You're not into the party scene?"

"Not really. I go to all the after-parties and everything because I don't want to be rude and sometimes it is nice to kick back and celebrate with friends, but my manager is the one who committed to me being here tonight."

I'll admit, I'm kind of surprised to hear her say that. The Chloe Conley that the media portrays is a huge party girl who loves to date around and will do just about anything for attention. This girl seems so... normal.

"I don't know if the guys' manager set this up or not," I tell her. "Even if he didn't, they were all so excited to be here tonight, they would have come anyway."

"They do know how to have a good time, don't they?" Chloe laughs.

"Oh, yeah." I have to agree.

Chloe sips at her drink, which is glowing a bright lavender under the lights. Then her expression softens a bit.

110

"Listen, I hope things didn't get too weird after what happened with Sam and me a few months ago. The media just takes everything so out of context. I never meant to stir up any drama for him or for Josh," she says.

"Oh, I know," I assure her. "Sometimes, I almost feel like we should all be used to it by now. But I remember how hard it was when people gossiped about me in high school. I can't imagine how it feels to have the entire world making up stories about you. And I'm sorry you all have to go through that."

Chloe shrugs. "It's a small price to pay for being able to do what I love. But I'm afraid of inadvertently screwing up other people's lives. You know what I mean?"

I think back to everything Sam has ever said to me about being afraid of how I'll be treated once people find out that we're dating. He even said to me once that he felt that he would be toxic to any girl he tried to go out with. That almost broke my heart.

"Yeah, I do."

As I reach for my drink, I notice a tall figure with curly hair approaching me out of the corner of my eye.

"Mel, there you are!" Oliver exclaims. "We've been looking all over for you. Sam's been trying to call you."

"Oh, has he?" I pull out my smart phone, but the battery is dead. "Well, that explains that."

"Hi, Oliver," Chloe greets him.

"Oh. Hello, Chloe. I'm sorry, I didn't see you there." Oliver is always so polite.

"No worries. It's kind of dark," Chloe replies.

"So, have the two of you been hanging out, then?" Oliver asks.

"Sort of. We just kind of ran into each other and started talking," I reply.

"Yeah, neither of us is really into the club scene," Chloe explains.

111

"That makes three of us," Oliver comments. "Did you come here alone, Chloe?"

"Yeah. The guy I've been seeing for a while got tired of never actually seeing me, so he ended it."

"Aw. I'm sorry to hear that," I tell her. I mean it. Chloe seems like a really sweet person.

"It was never very serious. There's just no time for that in this industry. I don't know how the two of you do it," she says.

"Who? Us?" I ask, indicating Oliver. "Oh, Chloe, we're not really together."

"You're not?"

"Nope. Just another rumor that got blown way out of proportion," I say.

"Ridiculous." Oliver shakes his head. "Not that you're not a lovely person, Mel. It's just..."

"I know. We're friends. It would be weird." Not to mention the fact that he knows that I'm madly in love with Sam and I know that he's madly in love with Joni. But even if I didn't know that, I still don't think there would be anything between us. Oliver is adorable, but I've never seen him as anything other than a friend.

"Oh my goodness, wow. I'm surprised. I really thought that was the one thing the press hadn't fabricated," Chloe remarks. "You would make a cute couple."

"Maybe, but as Sam pointed out, Oliver is British. He'd be cute with anybody," I tell her. At that, Chloe throws her head back and laughs.

"I'll give you that," she says.

Even in the fluorescent glow of blue and violet, I can tell Oliver is blushing. He'll never get used to girls fawning over him.

After I finish my Coke, I excuse myself to the restroom. Every other seat at the bar is occupied, so Oliver quickly claims mine.

112

As I should have been anticipating, the line to the ladies' room is so long, I'm really not sure if it's worth the wait. It might actually take less time to walk back to my hotel room a few blocks away and use my own toilet. But soon enough, the line is moving. Besides, I'd never make it more than a few meters in these heels.

Once I've finished, I try to find the clearest route back to the bar, where I hope Oliver and Chloe are still waiting for me. I try my best not to disturb anyone as I make my way through the crowds of drunken, dancing patrons.

Out of nowhere, I feel a large, rough hand grab me by the wrist. For a split second, I think it might be Sam, trying to get my attention before I disappear back into the masses. But after a brief moment of readjusting my eyes to the flashing lights around me, I realize that it isn't Sam. It's a man I don't know. He's older, probably early thirties, and he's tall, at least six feet. His dark hair is receding and he's sporting about a week's worth of a beard. But it's the way he looks me up and down with his beady eyes that makes my skin crawl.

"Where are you off to, Gorgeous?" he asks.

"I'm sorry. I have to go meet my friends." My answer is a rush, a fumbled mess of words.

"Whoa, whoa, slow down. No one is in a hurry around here. Now how about we try this again? I'm Tim. What's your name?"

"I can't. I really can't stay. My friends, they're waiting for me."

"Then let them wait. How about a dance?" Tim pulls me closer to him with a swift jerk of his arm. He's stronger than he looks.

"No. No, thank you." I try to shove my way out of his clutches, but his fingers are locked around my wrist.

"Come on. I bet I can show you a better time than they can," he mutters, reaching up to toy with a stray lock of my hair. I flinch before he can touch me.

"Please. Please, I really need to get going." Now I've resorted to begging. I look around at the people he's with, hoping that one of them will notice how uncomfortable he's making me, but they just laugh and keep on dancing. My captor, meanwhile, leans in and takes a deep breath.

"My God, you do smell amazing. You know, I think you and I should just - "

"Hey! What's going on here?"

And like a knight in shining armor, Sam appears, standing beside me, and staring the older man down with a look I can only describe as scathing. But it's not just him. It's all of them: Sam, Josh, Cory, even Jesse.

Tim seems neither impressed nor intimidated.

"Just asked a beautiful girl if she wanted a dance," he answers.

"Last time I checked, you didn't need to break her wrist in order to do so," Sam scowls.

"Yeah. Or touch her at all," Josh chimes in.

"What, are these guys your body guards?" Tim asks me.

"Actually, I'm her boyfriend, and I'd appreciate it if you'd take your filthy, drunken hands off her. Now," Sam demands.

My heart leaps into my throat as he speaks those words. Does he realize what he's saying? Or is he just trying to sound more threatening?

"Oh, really? She didn't mention that she had a boyfriend," Tim gloats. "Probably because she'd prefer a real man to a long-haired pretty boy with a - "

But before Tim can get the words out, Sam lunges at him, knocking the older man right off his feet. It doesn't take very long for onlookers with camera phones to start recording the star-studded scuffle unfolding on the dance floor. Oliver, Chloe, and Joni all show up as well, shouting above the ruckus, trying to figure out what's going on. All I care about is getting Sam out of there in one piece. And preferably not in handcuffs.

"Sam! Sam, it's okay!" I grab Sam by the elbow, hoping to break up the fight. "Sam, he's not worth it!"

Finally, he seems to hear me. Still shaking from the rush of adrenaline, and an uncharacteristic surge of anger, Sam stands up and takes me by the shoulders. His shirt is untucked and his hair is a glorious mess, but he seems to be stabilizing.

"Wow," Jesse remarks, eyeing all the spectators who are no doubt rushing to post images and videos of the brawl on all their respective social media sites. "I can't wait to see what the tabloids say tomorrow."

CHAPTER 13

"Birds and horses
Made of glass
Raindrops on your
Rose parade
Maybe home
Was never more
Than footprints
And the light of day..."

Song: "Home"
Artist: Morning Muses
From the Album: *Nightfall*

Breaking News: Sam Morneau Involved in Fist Fight!
Who knew the blue-eyed heartthrob had it in him? A video that surfaced in the early morning hours appears to show the twenty-year-old TKOS front man engaged in a full-out barroom brawl with another man. Eyewitness accounts claim that the man, who remains unidentified, was there with Morneau's ex-girlfriend, Chloe Conley. Is Sam's jealousy what drove Chloe away? Reps for both Morneau and Conley declined to comment.

"Well, it's about what we expected," Joni sighs.

It's the morning after the incident at Club Asteria and we're all exhausted. Sam, Cory, and Oliver stayed with Joni and me last night and none of us slept a wink. Oliver was worried about Joni, Cory was worried about all of us, and Sam... Sam just felt so terribly guilty.

He apologized over and over again, first for letting me out of his sight, and then for talking me into attending the opening in the first place. I tried to assure him that I wanted to go and that absolutely none of it was his fault. I think I've finally got him convinced, but it was a rough night for everyone involved.

On the bright side, I think I might have a new friend. I receive a text message shortly after the story from last night goes viral. It's from a number I don't know, but she identifies herself soon enough.

Hey Mel, it's Chloe. I asked Oliver for your number. I just wanted to say I'm sorry about what happened last night, and that I hope you're okay.

"Aw." I can't help but smile.

"What is it?" Joni asks.

"Chloe just sent me a text saying that she hopes I'm okay," I answer.

"Chloe? Chloe Conley?" Josh scowls. He still hasn't gotten over the rumors that spread about Chloe and him last year.

"Yeah. I talked to her for a bit last night. She's super sweet."

"Mel, how much did you have to drink last night? That girl isn't sweet!" Josh exclaims.

"Okay, what happened last year was not her fault. She has kind of a lousy manager," I tell him as I type out a response to Chloe.

Hi, Chloe. Thank you for your kind words. I'm fine. Sam and the guys are taking good care of me.

117

I'm glad you have such good friends in them. Tell them I said hello. It was fun talking to you last night! Hope we get to hang out again soon!

Seriously, that is one of the nicest things that anyone has ever said to me. I really like Chloe. Why couldn't Cory or Jesse have gone for someone like her?

I just hope that the TKOS fans aren't going to start harassing her again. Most of the fans are wonderful, but there is a small yet incredibly vocal minority that is very possessive of the guys, Sam especially. Any time he's reported to be dating someone, these fans start a regular online uprising. The guys have all asked them to stop and to show respect for their personal lives and the lives of others, but sadly, it continues.

I do, too! I tell her. *And listen, we're all sorry about the rumors going around. The guys will try to quell the media storm.*

Thank you. It's not too bad this time. I don't think people are taking these reports too seriously.

I'm happy to hear that, and hoping that she's right. I don't want Sam to feel even worse about all this. No matter how he's feeling, the guys still have a band rehearsal scheduled for this afternoon. It's one that I don't need to be at, which is nice since I really need to get caught up on my homework assignments, especially Statistics, which is kicking my butt even more than I thought it would at the beginning of the semester. I wish I could just take a nap instead, but for some reason, I'm still operating under the delusion that I can actually pass this class.

Joni, who, as I've mentioned before, is the smartest person in our little entourage, has helped me out a little, but she's been so busy these last few weeks that I've barely seen her at all. Stan and the rest of the managers are really keeping her on her toes this time around. It's been kind of nice, since it's given me a bit of extra time with Sam, but I do feel bad that she's having to work so much. It doesn't seem to bother

118

her, though, so I guess it shouldn't bother me. Besides, she gets to go with the guys to the rehearsal this afternoon while I stay holed up in our hotel room, crying over my Statistics homework, so you know, who's the real winner here?

Hint: it's not me.

...

"So, I just realized something," Sam announces. He and the guys finished rehearsing about an hour ago. While the rest of them retreated to Josh, Jesse, and Oliver's suite for some video gaming, Sam stopped by to help me with my homework. And by that I mean to distract me until I fail. Which will probably happen anyway without his help, but he seems determined to speed up the process.

"What's that?" I ask him, tapping my chin with my pencil's eraser.

"It's almost Valentine's Day."

Oh my goodness, he's right. I've been so distracted by statistics and rehearsals and life in general that I'd completely forgotten about the most romantic day of the year.

Okay, I actually don't think Valentine's Day is the most romantic day of the year. I usually associate it with boxes wrapped in pink and purple construction paper, cheap Ninja Turtles cards that you can buy by the dozen at the dollar store, and those little heart candies that taste like stale toothpaste. True, I usually buy myself a really big box of chocolate truffles every year which makes it worthwhile, but for the most part, Valentine's Day has never been that noteworthy in my book.

"It is, isn't it?" I ask.

"How should we celebrate?"

"Well, preferably alone." The last time we tried to have a date night, Josh showed up looking for his phone, noticed that we were watching one of his favorite movies, and decided to stick around. I'm sure there are several girls out there who would love to have Josh Cahill third-wheel it with them, but unfortunately, I am not one of them.

119

"Okay, so expectations are rather low. Good news for me," he teases.

"Sam we could literally spend our evening sitting around on the floor, in our sweat pants, eating Chinese food straight out of the container, and I would still think it was the best Valentine's Day ever." It's true. The older I get, the less I value extravagance and material gifts. It's all about moments and the people you share them with.

"I think we can at least make that *gourmet* Chinese food," Sam says.

"Fair enough."

"But really, you don't want to do something a bit more... romantic?" he asks. "You do know that money isn't an issue, right?"

"I know. And if I ever need a car or someone to bail me out of jail, trust me, you're going to be the first person I call."

"I'd better be." Sam grins and kisses me swiftly. "So what would you end up in jail for?"

"I don't know. Maybe arson after I light my statistics homework on fire and accidentally end up burning down the entire building?"

"Are you sure? I thought it was for stealing my heart."

"Oh, you did *not* just say that!" I exclaim, collapsing into a fit of giggles.

"Oh, but I did!" And then, Sam proceeds to snatch me up from my chair and drop me down onto my bed. "Drop out of school and run away with me!"

"I already did that!" I remind him.

It's kind of true. After high school graduation, I was all set to attend Cal State Long Beach and study graphic design, but Sam and his devastating charisma talked me into abandoning everything I thought I wanted and joining him and the guys on the road. It was a stupid gamble. The odds were a million to one that they'd actually make it. And yet, they did. It still blows my mind to think about it. That's why

120

I try to take everything in stride now. I'm not very good at it, but I'm learning.

"Well, drop out of statistics then! It's making you miserable and I don't like it when you're miserable. It makes me miserable."

God, could he be any more wonderful?

"Aw, I'm sorry I'm making you miserable." I reach up, running my hand through his soft blond locks and along his face.

"I'm sure you'll find a way to make it up to me," he murmurs, leaning down and planting a warm, gentle kiss on my mouth. Then his lips trail across my cheek, along my jaw line, and finally come to rest on my neck. I close my eyes and lose myself in his touch. After a few moments, he lays down next to me, presses his forehead to mine, and breathes a contented sigh. I open my eyes again and look at him.

For so many years, Sam has been the perfect guy to me, but I've never really taken the time to appreciate his little imperfections. Like the chicken pox scar to the side of his nose. Or the two golden brown freckles in his left iris. Or the fact that his two front teeth are just slightly crooked despite almost two years of braces. Somehow, all those minuscule imperfections make him even more perfect.

I'm not sure how long we lay there in silence before our eyes close and we drift off to sleep, but I'm very aware of how loud I yell when Joni barges into the room, waking both of us up and scaring me to death.

"What the hell, Mel?" Joni demands, switching the lights on. Sam and I must have slept longer than I thought. It was still daylight when I closed my eyes. Now the city outside my window is glowing against a backdrop of night sky and muted starlight.

"Sorry," I mutter, trying to catch my breath. "You startled me."

"Yeah, I kind of figured. What are you guys doing in here?"

121

"Taking a nap," Sam answers, stretching out his long arms and popping several vertebrae.

"Can't you nap in your own room?" Joni asks him.

"The napping wasn't planned, but then math happened and you know, sleeping is just so much better," Sam argues.

"Mel, you still haven't finished that homework? I thought I went over it with you," Joni scolds me.

"Not this stuff." And even if she did, I obviously forgot it. Math just doesn't stick in my brain. I'm better at remembering things like colors. Or really cool buildings.

"Oh, sorry. The managers have just been keeping me swamped," Joni sighs, kicking off her shoes and dropping her massive purse on her bed.

"Do you want me to have a talk with them?" Sam asks, looking concerned. "I had no idea they were working you this hard."

"No, it's alright. I really don't mind. It's just part of the business, you know?"

I actually don't know, because the managers don't expect nearly as much out of me as they do Joni. Maybe because I'm taking classes or maybe because I'm just not as much of a go-getter. Whatever the reason, I hope the managers know that they can come to me if they ever need anything extra done. I want to contribute and be a part of the team, and I know that I do and that I am, but I'm not as important or significant as Joni. I'm probably not supposed to think like that, but it's true.

"Anyway, Sam, would you mind going back to your own room? I kind of want to get ready for bed," Joni requests.

"Sure thing. I have a bag of chips and a few slices of leftover pizza calling my name anyway. Goodnight, girls."

Then, with one final secret smile, he leaves the room.

I must have a besotted look on my face, because Joni takes one look at me and says, "Do yourself a favor, Mel. Fall out of love with him."

122

"What?" *That* remark just totally threw me off my game. Or at least it would have if I had any game to begin with. "What is that supposed to mean?"

"It means, you're my best friend and I don't want to see you get hurt. Look, I know you like Sam and you have for years, but I just don't think he's the guy for you. You need someone a little more... conventional."

Her comment is so preposterous that I actually laugh right in her face. It's not even a normal laugh. It's more like an evil cackle.

"Conventional? You mean like a nice, typical, All-American guy with a nine-to-five job and a duplex? Where do you expect me to find one of those, Jo?"

"I didn't say you needed to find one now. I'm just saying that Sam Morneau isn't the type of guy you're going to end up with."

"Gee, thanks for that vote of confidence. What would I do without you?" I snap.

"Mel, I didn't mean it like that. Please, believe me, I'm only saying this for your own good. I don't want to see you investing your emotions in someone who isn't going to return them."

"And how do you know he isn't?" I can't believe we're having this discussion! This is as close to a fight as I've ever come with Joni. This isn't us!

Joni closes her eyes and sighs.

"I didn't want to have to tell you."

"Tell me what?" I ask.

Joni opens her eyes and looks at me again.

"My brother thinks that Sam might be seeing someone."

I can feel all the color fade from my face, but not for the reason that Joni suspects.

"Why does he think that?"

"The way he's been acting. And my brother found some a notebook of new lyrics that Sam left lying around. He

123

said they were really heartfelt. Almost sappy. It's not like the stuff that Sam usually writes," Joni explains. "I'm sorry Mel."

I try my best to look sad and not relieved, but truthfully, that isn't very much to go on. I do actually feel bad though, about being cross with Joni earlier. She was just trying to look out for me, after all. Even with all that she has on her shoulders, Joni Foreman is a really good friend.

"Thanks, Jo," I mumble, pulling my best sad face.

"You know I love you, right?" she asks.

"I do. And I love you, too," I tell her honestly. "Sorry I got a little snippy there."

"You're forgiven. I know how much you like Sam, and I'm sorry that it hasn't worked out for you yet." She pulls me into a sisterly embrace. "But you know, between you and me, I think you could do a lot better."

Again, I try my best not to react the way that I want to, which is something along the lines of hysterics mixed with love-drunk euphoria. There is no way I'll ever do better than Sam. It would simply be impossible, because for me, there is no one better than Sam.

But for now, I just smile.

"Thanks for looking out for me, Joni."

"Hey, you'd do the same for me."

She's right. I would.

And that's why I'm about to text Oliver.

CHAPTER 14

"And I'll be waiting for you
Where the lights can't find us
Hold your hands
Music surround us
After all this time
I'll make you my
Backstage Romance..."

Song: "Backstage Romance"
Artist: The Kind of September
From: Untitled Future Album

Okay, I might have gotten a little caught up in the best friends' moment, but I still think that texting Oliver and telling him about what a terrible time Joni has been having lately and suggesting he ask her out for Valentine's Day to make her feel better might be one of the best ideas I've ever had.

Oliver, bless his heart, is still a little shy around girls, and for the life of me, I can't figure out why! He's smart, he's sweet, he's funny, he's one of the cutest guys on the face of the planet, he's British... Honestly, he's got everything going for him! Not to mention that minor thing about being one fifth of the world's favorite boy band. You would think that would do at least a little something to boost his confidence around women!

Maybe it's being around guys like Josh and Jesse and even Sam who *know* they're good looking and *know* they're popular with the ladies. I guess next to them, anyone would feel a little insignificant. But Oliver deserves someone special. He deserves to be happy. And Joni deserves a fun night out with a cute British guy. So I'm hoping that he asks her and I'm especially hoping that she says yes.

Right now, I'm behind the scenes, watching a couple of internet journalists interview the guys for their Special Celebrity Valentine's Day podcast.

"So, let's settle those rumors once and for all. Of the five of you, how many *actually* have someone special in their lives?" the woman, Renee Sanders, asks. This question gets asked a lot.

"Cory," Josh and Sam answer together.

"Me," Cory affirms with a broad smile. "Tara and I have been together about four months now."

"Wow! Congratulations! And how's that going?" Marco White, Renee's cohost, asks, sounding intrigued.

"I've never been happier," Cory answers.

I notice Jesse shift in his seat and scowl off to the side. He can't possibly still be hung up on Tara, can he?

"And how about the rest of you? Any special ladies?" Adam asks.

"Nope. Just a group of eligible bachelors, living the good life," Josh answers, leaning back and stretching his arms out along the back of the couch.

"You mean the single life?" Sam asks.

"Exactly!"

"You mean to tell me that even with all those love songs that you write, none of you have any interest in dating?" Renee asks.

"Of course we do. As long as it's the right person," Sam answers.

"Okay, say you were to find that right person. How would you make their Valentine's Day special? What would you do?" Adam asks.

"I'd do something really extravagant. Like rent out a whole theme park. And then I'd take her out for a huge, five-course, gourmet meal," Josh says.

"Go big or go home, right?" Cory laughs.

"You got it, brother!"

"Oliver, we haven't heard very much from you. What would you do for your special someone on Valentine's Day?" Renee wonders.

"I don't know. Something a bit simpler. I'd want our evening to be a bit more intimate. Candles, chocolates, flowers...."

"Oliver's a bit old fashioned," Jesse remarks.

"He's British," Josh, Cory, and Sam all comment as one. Then they all laugh. Even Oliver cracks a smile.

"Alright, Jesse. Your turn," Adam says.

"Me? I'd tell her to decide. No better gift than giving the woman exactly what she wants."

"Okay, I can respect that. But you know, women also like to know that you've put some thought into making an evening special," Renee tells him. "Just speaking up for my fellow ladies."

"Well, why can't women take the initiative too? Why does it always have to be men?" Jesse asks.

"Yeah! I'd like to know the answer to that question," Josh says.

"So what you boys are saying is that you'd like a girl who takes charge? Who maybe asks *you* out?"

"Yeah!" Josh exclaims.

"Be careful what you wish for," Sam mutters playfully.

He's got a point. Josh is practically asking for it. Of course, it wouldn't be the first time.

"Okay, then, here's another question. What's the way to your heart? How would you want a girl to woo you?"

"Food," Josh answers automatically. "If you feed me, I'm yours."

"Just like a stray cat," Oliver teases.

"How about the rest of you?"

"For me, I just like a girl to be herself. To be open, honest," Sam answers. "I'm also a sucker for big brown eyes."

And now my cheeks are flushing pinker than a Valentine's Day heart.

"Oh thanks, now the rest of our answers are going to sound shallow," Jesse scolds Sam.

"But it's true!" Sam laughs.

"Jesse? What about you?" Renee asks.

"If a girl were really willing to take a risk to be with me... If she was willing to give it all up, whatever that may be. I'd know she was the one," Jesse answers.

"Wow. How very *Romeo and Juliet* of you, Jess," Josh snickers. Jesse just shrugs.

"Okay, last question. Cory, since you are the only one in a relationship, what are your Valentine's Day plans?" Adam asks.

"I can't give you all the details, because it's a surprise for Tara, but I can tell you that it's going to be very romantic... and very tropical."

I'm going to be petty and admit that I hate the fact that someone as nice as Cory is putting so much effort into making Valentine's Day so lovely and beachy for someone as horrible as Tara. But at least that means that Sam will get his hotel room all to himself for a few days. It will be nice to be able to enjoy Valentine's Day without having to worry about Cory coming home early.

After the interview ends, I catch up with Oliver.

"Hey!" I greet him, tugging on his sleeve. "So, have you decided yet?"

"What?" he asks.

"Whether or not you're going to ask Joni out for Valentine's Day."

"Well, you see, I kind of already did."

I can't help it. I squeal.

"Oh my God, really? Oh Oliver, that's so exciting! So what are you going to do?"

"She said no."

My heart stutters then comes to a screeching halt.

"Wait, what?"

"She said that it was very nice of me to ask, but she has to work all Valentine's Day weekend."

"But that's not fair!" I cry out, far more upset over Joni's rejection than even Oliver seems. But I can't help it. I feel terrible! I'm the one who encouraged Oliver to ask her out and now not only does she know that he has feelings for her, but she's broken his heart, too? This wasn't supposed to happen! They were supposed to have the greatest Valentine's Day ever.

Oliver simply shrugs. "It's not something that can be helped."

I guess he's got a point. And it's not like she turned him down because she's not interested. With Joni, work always comes first. I guess that's admirable, but if you ask me, it's no way to live. Especially when she could be going out with Oliver Berkley.

Back at the hotel, I approach Sam with my woes.

"I just can't believe they're making her work on Valentine's Day! They couldn't give her one night off?"

"Yeah, about that..." Sam begins.

"What? Oh, please don't tell me we have to work on Valentine's Day too!"

"No, it's not that. It's just that Oliver told me what Joni said, so I took it upon myself to have a chat with Stan."

129

"And?"

"He had no idea what I was talking about. According to him, there have been no extra meetings, no overtime, nothing."

"But... how is that possible? We've seen how preoccupied Joni's been lately."

"She might be preoccupied, but it isn't with work."

Now I'm more curious than ever. Something is clearly going on, something that Joni doesn't want us to know about. I pull out my phone.

Hey, where are you? I text her.

In a meeting, but I'll be back in about an hour.

Oh my God! That is a boldfaced lie. My best friend just texted a lie right to my face! True, I haven't been one hundred percent honest with her, but I try to make a point to not tell outright fibs. Mine are more lies of omission, which, technically are still lies. But still. I'm affronted by her gall.

When she shows up in our hotel room an hour later Sam and I are both waiting to interrogate her.

"Hey." Her greeting is innocent enough. She obviously doesn't suspect a thing. "How was the interview?"

"It was fine. Don't change the subject," Sam snaps.

Joni looks confused and mildly alarmed.

"I didn't change the subject. There was no subject."

"Don't care." Sam waves her comment aside. "We're onto you."

"What are you talking about?"

Sam looks at me.

"Do you want to tell her, Mel, or should I?"

"Tell me what?" Joni persists.

I take a step toward her and cross my arms.

"We know you haven't actually been going to meetings," I tell her.

"Yeah. Or working overtime," Sam adds.

"What? How did you find out?" Joni asks.

"Not important!" Sam exclaims.

"Sam went to have a talk with Stan after you told Oliver that you had to work on Valentine's Day. He didn't think it was fair to expect so much of you," I explain.

"Yeah. Especially since Valentine's Day is on a Sunday," Sam tells her, acting for all the world like an irritated dad who's just caught his daughter sneaking out on a school night. "So, Miss Foreman, spill."

For the first time since I've known her, Joni looks genuinely caught off guard. Her eyes are wide and she seems to be fighting an impulse to run away. She's so nervous, she's making *me* anxious.

Finally, she sighs. "Okay, fine. I've been seeing someone."

"What?" Sam and I both gasp.

"Who? How long? Do we know him?" I ask.

"I guess you'll find out sooner or later," she answers. "It's Chris."

Chris? Chris who? We only know one Chris. Chris Ortega. And he totally has a girlfriend.

"Chris?" Sam asks, echoing my thoughts. "Chris as in our drummer, Chris?"

"Yes!" Joni sounds exasperated, like she can't figure out why we're not understanding her.

"But what about Angela?" I wonder. Chris and Angela have been together for as long as I've known them. Wouldn't I have heard if they'd broken up? Wouldn't we all have heard?

"They'd been on the rocks for a while and she finally ended it last October."

"What?!" Sam and I yelp again.

"Why didn't he tell us? I thought they were still together!" I say.

"It was really rough on him and he didn't want to talk about it. He knows how fast gossip spreads in this circle and he just didn't want to make it a big deal," Joni explains.

"But he told you?" Sam asks.

131

"I noticed he was down one day and we went out to coffee. We started talking more... He's a really great guy," Joni tells us, a slow smile spreading across her pretty face.

I can't believe it! Joni has had a secret boyfriend for months and I didn't know about it?! Okay fine, my secret boyfriend is standing right next to me and she still doesn't know about him. But it's kind of something that I would expect from someone like me. Joni on the other hand is so up front and honest and level-headed. Running around and having a secret romance with a drummer isn't exactly her style. But she's clearly been enjoying it.

"Wait a minute, what about all your talk about not wanting to date a musician?" I ask her.

"What do you mean?" Joni asks.

"I mean for the past year, all I've heard from you is how you could never date a musician and that musicians are just the worst and you could never be with someone who's always in the public eye," I remind her. It's true. Ever since she broke up with Jesse, Joni has been *very* vocal about her feelings towards musicians.

"Ouch," Sam remarks.

"What I meant was that I didn't want to have a high profile relationship," Joni says. "Come on, you know what it's like. We can't even be seen with one of the guys without someone starting up a rumor that we're in a relationship. I don't want that."

"Again, ouch."

"Oh, shut up, Sam," Joni snaps.

"So why didn't you tell any of us?" I ask her.

"I guess I wanted to see where it was going. You know me, Mel. I'm terrible at relationships. I didn't want to get my hopes up or make it seem like a bigger deal than it was. I guess I just... really didn't want to jinx things."

I guess it really shouldn't surprise me that Joni is self-conscious when it comes to relationships. Of course, I blame Jesse for that. Joni is intelligent and beautiful and independent and probably one of the strongest women I know. She has absolutely no reason to doubt herself. Then again, I know how she feels. I have my own insecurities. I'm not as pretty or smart or brave as I would like to be. But I know that Sam loves me in spite of all that. That's the best part about falling in love with your best friend.

"Well, if it makes you feel better, your secret is safe with us," I assure her.

"Thank you, Mel."

"She's actually devastated on the inside," Sam quips.

Joni and I both stare at him.

"What does that mean?" Joni asks.

"You know. Her thing for drummers..." Sam teases, looking so very amused with himself.

I feel my jaw drop. Seriously? He's really going to do this right now?

"Mel, you have a thing for drummers?" Joni asks.

Oh, great. She really hasn't heard this joke before? Sam makes it *all* the time.

"I do *not* have a thing for drummers."

"You didn't have feelings for Chris, did you?" Now Joni looks genuinely concerned.

"Oh, my God, no! I do not have feelings for Chris. I don't have a thing for drummers!" How many times do I have to say this?

"Okay, if you're sure," Joni says.

"Jo, come on. Since when do you take anything he says seriously?" I ask, indicating Sam.

"Good point."

"Hey, I can be serious. Watch." Sam clears his throat, pauses, then collapses into a fit of giggles. "I'm sorry, I just can't do it."

Joni looks at me.

"And you wonder why I don't want to date *that*."

CHAPTER 15

"Let me tell you what I'm thinkin' about
A sunset drive with the windows down
I feel that fire in my soul
As I listen to some classical rock and roll
And this whole time I've been away
I still haven't forgotten the words you say
But you're not coming back and it's better this way..."

Song: "Forget"
Artist: The Kind of September
From the Album: *Meet Me on the Midway*

It's February 14th. Valentine's Day is officially upon us.

Cory and Tara have been in Bermuda for a few days now. I'm glad I didn't have to see her. Thankfully, my face has healed up nicely since she shoved me in the supply closet. We've pretty much avoided each other since that incident.

Jesse, meanwhile, has been sulking nonstop ever since that interview the guys gave a few days ago. He finally seems to be living up to that broody bad boy image. It's about to drive all of us crazy. I can't bring myself to believe that he is actually that torn up over the likes of Tara Meeks, but apparently his feelings for her were pretty strong. That, or he's just jealous that Tara picked Cory over him, if that is indeed how it all went down. I didn't ask. I've just gone about my business like nothing ever happened.

Hopefully going out with Josh and Oliver back to Club Asteria tonight will do him some good. Sam made up the excuse that he wanted to stay home and relax instead of venturing back out to the club where he almost got himself banned for tackling a fellow patron. Of course, no club owner in their right mind would ban Sam Morneau, or any other member of a popular band.

Speaking of Oliver, I haven't had the heart to tell him the truth about Joni, who will be spending her Valentine's Day with Chris at an undisclosed location.

Joni is absolutely glowing. Although her confession stunned me, I've got to admit I've never seen her this happy. Chris seems really good for her. And she seems good for him too. I've always thought Chris was a pretty cool guy, but I've never really gotten to know him on a really personal level. After spending a bit of time with him and Joni, I've come to find he's really courteous, even chivalrous. It's funny, because when you look at Chris, you don't think *gentleman*. You think *rock star*. He's tall and burly with unkempt dark hair and lots of tattoos. He wears torn jeans, vintage t-shirts, and I've never seen him without a red plaid bandana tied around his head. But he's as kind and generous and polite as they come.

Who knew?

That just leaves Sam and me. I have no idea what he has planned. All I know is that I'm supposed to meet him in his room at eight o'clock. That gives me plenty of time to prepare a few Valentine's Day surprises of my own.

Sam loves homemade desserts, especially brownies, so I spend a good portion of my afternoon baking. He's also a big fan of zombies, so I bought him the *The Walking Dead* graphic novel box set. I know for a fact he doesn't have it, not because he doesn't read, but because he really doesn't have time to. Since we'll be spending so much time on the road beginning in just a few short weeks, however, maybe he'll have a little down time on the bus.

After I'm finished baking, I take a quick shower and change into a gray dress with a red belt and red heels to match. I also have silver heart earrings that my mother gave me in high school. They're a little cliché, I admit, but you know, sometimes I kind of like cliché.

Grabbing the brownies and the gift bag containing his new books, I walk down to Sam's room and knock quietly on the door. He answers, looking handsome as ever in dark jeans and a blue button-down shirt.

"Happy Valentine's Day," I greet him.

"Happy Valentine's Day to you," he replies, inviting me inside. Once he closes the door, he takes my waist and kisses me on the lips. Then, he glances down at the items in my hands. "Oh, Melissa Parker, you really do love me, don't you?"

Like I said, baked desserts are probably his favorite thing in the entire world.

"I do," I tell him. "You wouldn't give me any clues about what we were doing tonight, but I figured no matter what, we could always enjoy brownies."

"You are correct. And what's that?" he asks, indicating the bag.

"I don't know. I guess you'll have to open it."

"Before I do that," Sam scampers around to the other side of his bed, reaches down, and emerges with a single red rose and a small turquoise box with a white ribbon. "I should let you open yours as well."

Inside the box is a simple, delicate, and breathtakingly elegant silver necklace with a single, sparkling diamond pendent.

"Oh, Sam," I breathe.

"I know you don't like gaudy jewelry, so I thought that was perfect. Pure and beautiful. Like you."

"Will you help me put it on?"

"Of course."

I pull my long hair off to the side as Sam fastens the clasp at the nape of my neck. Then, he lets his fingers trail down my back before he leans in and kisses the curve of my shoulder. I try not to shiver.

Finally, I turn around to watch him open his gift. His face lights up when he sees the gruesome, decaying zombie on the cover.

"Aw, wow! This is perfect! Thank you!" He pulls me into a long embrace. "You're the best girlfriend ever, you know that?"

"I try," I smile and rise up on my toes to steal another kiss. Even in heels, I'm much shorter than he is.

Within a few minutes, our dinner arrives. He's ordered in from our favorite local Thai food restaurant, incidentally the same meal we ate the night he and I first got together. I wonder if he remembers that or if he just picked Thai food because he knows we both love it so much.

We make small talk over dinner, mostly about the upcoming tour and how excited we both are. We're set to visit cities that we've never seen before, including New Orleans and Seattle. With two world tours behind us, it's weird to think that there are places like that, especially where music is so prominent, that we haven't seen. But there are only so many cities we can visit in a year.

Once we've finished eating, he checks his new smart watch (which I think is kind of silly but he absolutely loves because he says it makes him feel like he's in an intergalactic sci-fi movie) and says, "Right on time."

"For what?" I ask.

"You'll see," he grins. "Are you about ready to head out?"

"We're going somewhere?" I ask.

"Of course. Did you think this was it?" he laughs.

"Well, this has been very nice!" I would have been totally fine if this *was* it. It's been a wonderful evening so far. I'm with the love of my life, we just ate an amazing dinner, and there isn't a single toothpaste-flavored candy heart in sight. This is the best Valentine's Day I've ever had.

"It has been nice," he agrees. "But this is no ordinary date night."

At first, I'm not sure what to think. What does he have planned? Are we really going to leave the hotel? What if we get caught? It's one thing to be seen in public together, hanging out in our home town, but to be seen driving around, dressed up, looking very much like we're on a date, on *Valentine's Day*? That might be just a little conspicuous.

Especially if we're driving around in the sleek black Porsche that Sam has rented for the evening.

"Are you for real?" I gape at the luxury car as Sam opens the passenger door for me.

"Most of the time," Sam winks.

As expected, traffic on Highway 101 is a nightmare, but once we make it to open road, Sam rolls the windows down and turns the music on the radio up. I laugh as the night wind rushes through my hair and Sam sings at the top of his lungs. It's one of those rare, perfect moments of existence. I feel invincible. I feel like I'll never come down from the high that I'm on. Nothing in the world can touch me.

Once we exit onto a smaller, quieter street, however, he rolls the windows back up and turns the radio down.

"Don't want to draw attention to ourselves, do we?" he grins.

"So, where exactly are we going?" I ask him. Thanks to LA traffic, we've already been driving for half an hour.

"You'll see." I knew he wasn't actually going to tell me. Why did I even bother?

138

After a few more minutes, we leave the residential streets and gas stations and fast food restaurants and we continue venturing north into a beautiful wooded area. Just barely, I can make out the rolling California hills in the distance. It's so peaceful out here at night, a welcome escape from the busy city.

"Are we getting close?" I ask.

By now, all signs of parking lots and lamp posts have disappeared, and Sam is carefully navigating the Porsche along the winding mountain roads.

"Perhaps."

Finally, he pulls into an empty parking lot on top of a hill. Directly ahead of us, a magnificent white building with three black domes is lit up against the night sky.

The Griffith Observatory.

"Surprised?" Sam asks, his eyes alight with excitement.

"What are we doing here?" I ask him.

"Stargazing, I presume. We might also eat some of those delicious brownies you made."

"But... I meant... It's after hours. We can't get in."

At that, Sam looks offended. Comically so.

"Have you forgotten who you're here with?" he asks, climbing out of the car. "Believe it or not, there are a few advantages to being Sam Morneau."

"But... how?"

"I made a phone call. Pulled a few strings," he shrugs. "So, what do you think?"

"I'm speechless," I admit, taking his hand.

"Don't you mean star struck?" he grins.

"Bad."

It's amazing the kind of difference a little distance can make. In the heart of Los Angeles, you have little hope of ever seeing past all the light pollution. But out here in the mountains, the galaxies dance before my eyes in a symphony of starlight. The sight takes my breath away.

When we reach the Observatory, Sam introduces himself to the night guard, who graciously lets us in with a simple, "Enjoy your evening."

Since the exhibits and the planetarium are closed for the evening, Sam immediately leads me out to the observation deck.

"Sorry we can't see all of it, but this is what I really had in mind," he tells me as I take my first look out over the horizon.

The sparkling sea of city lights below us is surreal. It all seems so big and daunting when you're a part of it, but when you're looking down on it, especially from such an amazing place with such an amazing person, its significance kind of fades away. In fact, everything fades away. I wish everyone in the world could see what I'm seeing right now.

I don't know how long we stand there in silence. Even though we're watching the world move beneath us, for me, it feels like time is standing still.

"It's kind of nice to get away from it all," Sam murmurs into my hair.

"It is," I agree. "This is perfect, Sam."

"I'm glad you like it."

Then, he pulls out his smart phone and sets it on the ledge. A slow, acoustic ballad begins to play. He looks at me and silently extends his hand. I take it without hesitation. My heart races as he pulls me into a close embrace and places his other hand on the small of my back. I rest my head on his chest and listen to his heart beating. It's quite possibly my favorite sound in the world.

"You know if there's one thing I regret," he tells me, "it's never taking you to a real dance."

"You mean like in high school?" I ask.

He nods. "I know we went a few times in groups, but I should have taken you to Prom our senior year. Instead, I had you halfway across town in one of the shadiest concert venues in the state of California."

"I chose to be there," I remind him. "Besides, I think you've made up for it."

"Yeah?" he asks, grinning down at me.

"Oh yeah," I assure him. "This is way better than Prom."

"Good," he smiles. Then he kisses me. And again. And again.

Perhaps it's his warm embrace, or the sheer divinity of the stars and planets surrounding us, but suddenly, I hear myself whisper, "I think we should tell them."

"Tell who?" Sam asks.

"Our friends. I want to tell them about us."

"Are you sure?"

"I don't want them to find out the way that we found out about Joni and Chris, after an interrogation and being caught in a lie. I love you, Sam, and I don't want to keep pretending that I don't. You're my favorite person in the world."

Sam looks overwhelmed, almost bashful, which is very uncharacteristic of him.

"So are you," he replies. "If you're sure about this, we'll tell them. First thing in the morning. Tonight, I just want it to be you and me."

I wrap my arms around his neck and pull him into another kiss. I swear, I can feel the stars falling down around us.

"That is fine by me."

CHAPTER 16

"And I think we should take a little time
To enjoy the summer breeze
Raindrops on the windshield
Your lips upon my cheek
Just take a little time
To enjoy these simple little moments
Remember to stop and breathe
Because once you're in the city
Baby, you'll never want to leave..."

Song: "The City"
Artist: Chloe Conley
From the Album: *Chloe*

The next morning, I wake up in Sam's arms. It's the first night we've ever spent together. Like this. Alone. And it was perfect. True, he's still a bit of a tosser-turner and my goodness, that boy is a chatter-box when he falls asleep, but all of that meant that I was really with him. And I wouldn't have had it any other way.

I knew Joni wouldn't be back. She texted me while Sam and I were still at the Observatory.

Spending tonight with Chris. Don't wait up!

So here we are. Sam is still asleep. His dark blond hair is spread out all over the place on my pillow and he's breathing deeply through lips that are just barely parted. He's shirtless, which gives me a clear view of the tattoos on his chest and upper arms. A lion. An anchor. A compass. A crown. His father's name, Thomas. His mother's name, Laurel. An owl. A tree. Deftly, I run my fingers along the tree's outstretched branches. Sam stirs at my touch and opens sleepy blue eyes.

"Hey," he grins, his voice lower and much quieter than usual.

"Hi," I reply and kiss him lightly.

"How'd you sleep?"

"Pretty well. You?"

"Like a rock," he answers, pulling me into a tight, warm embrace. "So. Are you ready to break the news?"

"Maybe you should let me brush my teeth first," I murmur into his neck.

"Yeah, you probably need it," he teases. I kick him playfully in retaliation.

While I brush my teeth and get dressed, Sam actually retreats back to his room for a quick shower. When he arrives back at my door fifteen minutes later, smelling like spearmint toothpaste and Old Spice shampoo, he smiles and offers his hand.

"Shall we?" he asks.

Heart thudding with anticipation, I take his hand and lace my fingers through his, and together, we walk down the hall toward the room where the rest of his bandmates are staying. Sam gives their secret knock on the door and we both wait for Josh or Oliver or Jesse to answer and see that we're holding hands.

But that doesn't happen.

143

Oliver answers, looking terribly preoccupied, almost troubled, and greets us with a very distracted, "Hey," without even looking at us.

It's only after he retreats back inside that I notice the fourth person in the room. Cory, who, last time I checked, was supposed to be in Bermuda with Tara. Not hunched over on an ottoman in his friends' hotel room.

"Cory? What are you doing here?" Sam asks. "I thought you weren't coming back until tomorrow."

"Clearly, you haven't checked Twitter in the last twelve hours," Josh remarks.

By now, Sam and I have let go of each other's hand. Something isn't right. Cory wouldn't just drop everything with Tara and fly home unless there was a real emergency. Is it Joni? Was there an accident last night? Or what if it's someone back home?

"No, we both crashed pretty early last night," Sam tells them. "Is everything okay?"

"It's over," Cory mumbles. He sounds like he's been crying. In all the years I've known him, I think I've only seen Cory cry once, and that was the night the last *Harry Potter* book was released. He's a bit emotionally invested.

"What is?" I ask.

"Tara. We're done."

I'm stunned, partly because of how abruptly the romance ended, partly because Sam and I somehow managed to avoid hearing about it for twelve hours, and partly because I'm actually kind of sad. Not because I'll never have to see Tara again. That comes as a *huge* and very welcome relief. But because of how sad Cory is. I don't like seeing any of my friends hurting, particularly one whom I've regarded for many years as a brother.

"Oh my God, Cory. I'm sorry," I tell him, kneeling down in front of him and taking his hand. "Are you okay?"

"No," he grumbles. "She cheated on me."

144

"What?" And just like that, my heart is racing with a whole new kind of dread and anticipation. How did he find out? Did she tell him? Does he know it was with Jesse? Does he know that I know? I'm too afraid to ask.

"How do you know?" Sam asks.

"It broke last night around nine o'clock our time," Jesse explains. "All over social media. Gossip columns. Tabloids. You name it."

"I don't understand." By now, I'm trembling. Why is Jesse so calm? If reports of Tara's affair have spread this quickly, it's only a matter of time before someone wants to know who she cheated with! It's almost impossible to keep anything private once the internet becomes involved.

"At first, I thought nothing of it, just the usual stupid gossip. But then it began to spread and it got bigger and bigger... When I asked Tara about it, she tried to deny it, but she was panicked. Her eyes went wide. I knew then, just by looking at her face, that it was true." Poor Cory! He sounds absolutely devastated.

"And she won't tell you who the other party involved is?" Oliver asks tentatively.

"She tried to convince me it was just a one-time thing, but I know she's lying. According to the source, she was with the other guy for months," Cory replies.

Right now, it is all I can do to not hightail it out of the room. I feel so, so guilty. I should have said something earlier, put a stop to it when I had the chance. But I didn't and now my friend is heartbroken and it's indirectly my fault. Because I knew and I did nothing. I willingly let Cory continue on in a relationship I knew wasn't right for him, with a woman I knew was unfaithful to him. What kind of friend does that make me?

A pretty rotten one, that's what.

"Sucks, man," Josh tells him.

"At least you found out now, before the tour starts," Sam offers. "It'll give you some time to get over her."

"I don't want to get over her. I loved her. I thought she loved me." Cory hangs his head and wipes at his nose with his sleeve.

"Hey, where's Joni?" Oliver asks out of nowhere.

"Uh..." This is a problem. Because no matter what I tell them, something isn't going to add up. If I say she's still asleep, someone will point out that Joni is the only early-bird amongst us and if we're all awake, then she's awake. If I say that I haven't seen her, someone will wonder where exactly she is and might even figure out that she didn't come home last night. If I tell them the truth, well, that's just another bombshell to add to an already overwhelming series of events. "I don't know. Probably off running errands or meeting with Stan."

Huh, that lie came almost naturally. Not sure that's a good thing.

"I'm guessing she hasn't heard about this either, then," Josh comments. "If she had, she'd be demanding Tara's head be brought to her on a wooden stake."

This is very true. I pull out my phone just the same, however, to see if she's tried to contact me. She hasn't. Out of sheer curiosity, I log in to Twitter to see exactly what people have been saying about Tara. It isn't pretty.

HOW COULD TARA DO THIS TO CORY I AM LITERALLY SO MAD I CAN'T SEE STRAIGHT #SUPPORTCORY

@ItsTaraMeeks has pissed off an ENTIRE FANDOM. I would be very afraid if I were her right now. #SeptembristsUnite

Can we please stop talking about She-Who-Must-Not-Be-Named and instead focus on Cory and how he must be feeling right now?

But seriously WHO would cheat on @CoryTKOS? He is the sweetest, cutest, most innocent person ALIVE! #WeLoveYouCory

Tara Meeks has broken our perfect Cinnamon Roll's heart. She will pay for this. #DestroyTara #SupportCory

146

Tara, meanwhile, has deactivated her account. I can't say I blame her. There is only way to draw more negative attention to yourself than to date a member of The Kind of September, and that's to break one of their hearts. Their fans may be a little crazy, possessive even, but they are *very* protective of their boys. If anyone or anything were to ever threaten The Kind of September, you can bet your life they'd have an army of fangirls standing in their way.

Meanwhile, news is spreading amongst our other friends. I just received a text from Chloe.

I just heard about Cory and Tara! Is he okay?

I write back, *Not really. But we're all with him.*

Well, between you and me, I think he's better off without her. She seemed kind of mean.

Yeah, that's definitely one word for her. I could come up with a few others, but they're far less polite.

Josh doesn't seem to have a problem listing them, however. I've only been listening with one ear, but I've definitely heard the words, "Selfish bitch" and "Troll-faced ho."

"Josh, do you really think that's helping?" Oliver asks quietly.

"It's making me feel better." Josh crosses his arms over his chest.

"Maybe you should try to get in touch with Joni," Sam mutters in my ear.

"I think maybe you're right," I tell him.

I excuse myself, walk out into the hall, and press the *Call* button next to Joni's name in my phone. It rings several times before connecting to voicemail. I hang up and dial again. I know Joni. Her phone is never beyond her reach. She even takes it into the bathroom when she showers. And I know for a fact that she sleeps with the volume on because her stupid ring tone has woken me up more times than my actual alarm. I swear, I have a Pavlovian reaction now every time I hear the first few notes of "Pachelbel's Canon."

This time, she answers. She probably ignored it the first time when she saw that it was me. But to be fair, if she called me while I was alone with Sam, I'd probably let it go to voicemail too.

"Hello?" Her voice is hoarse. I definitely just woke her up. Karma.

"Hey, Jo, where are you?"

"Still with Chris. We got a room in a hotel down the street. Why?"

"Cory flew home last night. He and Tara broke up. He's pretty upset."

There's a moment of silence on Joni's end before I hear her victory cry.

"YES!" she exclaims. "Sorry, I know that sounds really insensitive, but thank GOD. Oh, this really was the best Valentine's Day ever."

"Joni, look, I know you're happy she's gone, and trust me, I am too, but I think Cory could really use his sister right now. And not the See-I-Told-You-She-Was-Terrible sister. The warm and loving and compassionate one."

"Okay, yeah, I'll be there soon. Just tell me one thing, Mel. What finally made him see the light?" Joni asks.

This one, I'm hesitant to answer. But she's going to find out sooner or later.

"Tara cheated on him."

Joni heaves a frustrated sigh.

"I knew it. I knew she was rotten. I knew she was only using him to get famous and that she was a liar and a phony and of course, she turned out to be a cheater too. God, I hate that girl."

"I think the entire world is with you on that one."

"Wait a minute, has this spread?" Joni asks.

"Oh yeah."

"Great. That means we're going to be dealing with dozens, possibly hundreds of reporters trying to get the inside scoop and documenting every moment of my brother's heartbreak."

"We'll deal with all that later. Right now, we just need to take care of Cory," I remind her.

"You're right. Stay with him till I get there, will you?"

"We all will."

"Thanks, Mel. You're a good friend."

Her words cut deep into my already riddled conscience.

If only she knew.

CHAPTER 17

"After nightfall
We'll get away
Through these empty
Backstreet alleys
I feel your heartbeat
Stop and breathe
Everything will
Be okay tonight..."

Song: "Nightfall"
Artist: Morning Muses
From the Album: *Nightfall*

It's Over: Cory Foreman and Tara Meeks SPLIT!
Cory Vows to Find Tara's Mystery Man!
Tara CHEATED on Cory... And Septembrists are
Plotting Revenge!
Tara Meeks is learning the hard way that you don't mess
with The Kind of September... or their legions of dedicated fans.
According to a source close to the model, she engaged in a months-
long romance with another man - WHILE she was dating the TKOS

hottie. The source failed to identify the man, but rumors have begun circulating that it may have been someone in the band's inner circle! Talk about betrayal! The one light at the end of this devastating tunnel of heartache? Cory Foreman is officially back on the market!

Okay, so here's how it all went down.

Cory and Tara were having a wonderful time in Bermuda, snorkeling, playing with dolphins, and publicly displaying their affection for one another in full view of the trailing paparazzi. We all know this because photographs of them making out in the surf are all over the internet this morning, along with the scathing headlines.

Anyway, Tara must have found out about the rumors before Cory, because he said that she started acting really anxious. She didn't even gloat when a few fans stopped and asked to take pictures with them. That's just not like her. She's a big fan of fake modesty. You know, like when someone pretends to complain but they're actually bragging? *Oh, I just can't go anywhere without someone stopping me for an autograph! It's exhausting!* That is classic Tara.

At first, Cory said that he thought she may have been feeling sick from the shrimp and calamari that they'd eaten the night before. She had mentioned that it tasted a little off. Of course, that was probably just her *actually* complaining. Is nothing ever good enough for that girl?

That's when Cory's phone started going crazy with text messages, some from people he doesn't even know that well, asking what was going on. They told him that both he and Tara were trending topics on Twitter. The rest is history.

Tara tried to deny it at first. She reminded him of the lies that the press loved to tell about anyone in the public eye, even his own bandmates. Especially his bandmates! Why should he expect them to treat his girlfriend with even an ounce of dignity? But he finally broke her down. I guess she must have cared about him at least a little bit if she respected him enough to be honest with him. I just wonder *how* honest she was.

151

Cory clearly doesn't know that Jesse was the one she cheated with, and for the life of me, I can't figure out why Tara didn't sell him out. Is it because she's hoping to reconcile with Cory? Or maybe Jesse? I've been trying to get a moment alone with him, Jesse I mean, to find out if he knows anything or if Tara's tried to contact him, but I haven't had the chance.

Joni is on an absolute rampage. She's thrilled that Tara is out of her brother's life, but she's also furious that she broke Cory's heart. That fury far outweighs any feelings of happiness or triumph that she might be feeling over never having to see or deal with Tara again.

"I just don't know what makes me angrier, the fact that she actually *cheated* on my brother, or the fact that he liked her so much that it actually makes him *sad* that she cheated on him. And you know what's even worse? All the publicity that she's gaining from this mess!" Joni ranted to me last night before bed.

"But it's really, really bad publicity," I reminded her.

"Mel, how long have you been in this business? There is *no such thing* as bad publicity. Not to women like her who only care about being the center of attention! She might be getting some *negative* publicity, but as far as she's concerned, that is only going to boost her career in the long run. She's probably soaking up every moment of this because everyone is talking about her."

That might have been true, but I've seen some of the things that people have been writing about her. One article referred to her as "*The most hated woman on the internet*." That has to hurt at least a little bit.

Then Joni said something that really got me thinking.

"I bet she did it."

"Did what?" I wondered.

"I bet Tara leaked the story herself. She's probably been planning this since she and Cory first got together."

"That doesn't make sense."

"Mel, think about it! We both know that Tara was never actually interested in Cory. Girls like her don't go for guys like my brother. They go for guys like Sam. Or Jesse." I might have been insulted had it not been for the fact that she was absolutely dead on. Tara may have been seeing Cory out in the open, but Jesse was the one she chose behind closed doors. "Tara was only dating Cory because she knew that he was crazy about her. The way he fawned over here? She *thrives* on stuff like that. The only other thing he had going for him was that he was already famous, exactly the kind of famous that she wanted to be. And what better way to get famous than to date a famous person?"

"But to leak her own affair? Are you sure she's smart enough for that?" To me, Joni's thought process was pretty convoluted, but then again, it was almost midnight and I was exhausted.

"No, but I'm certain she's evil enough for that. For all we know, she didn't even *have* an affair. Maybe Cory was getting too wishy washy for her, what with the stupid trip to Bermuda."

"I wouldn't dump Cory if he took me to Bermuda." That's the last thing I remember saying. By that point, I was pretty much sleep-talking.

Now it's the morning after and Joni hasn't come forth with any more conspiracy theories. Just non-stop ranting about all the bad things she hopes happen to Tara, including but not limited to unemployment, female-patterned baldness, and leprosy. A bit harsh, but I can't say I'd feel any different if I found out a girl broke my brother's heart. Of course, Aidan is only seven, so I'm hoping he still has a long way to go before I have to worry about that.

As far as Cory is concerned, I really don't think Joni's endless list of insults and ill-will to the girl he used to love is helping him much. It actually seems to be upsetting him more. But none of us are brave enough to point that out to Joni when she's in Protective Sister Mode. Cory and Joni might not always see eye-to-eye, but Joni can be downright vicious when it comes to protecting him. It's sweet, even if she is a little scary.

I'm just glad the guys don't have anything scheduled for today. I honestly don't know if Cory could handle an interview or a photo shoot right now. We're all back in Jesse, Oliver, and Josh's room and Cory is sitting on the floor, staring glumly into nowhere. He looks absolutely pitiful. Josh has already made the mistake of trying to cheer him up by offering to take him to a strip club. Cory actually looked offended. No one's tried to cheer him up since. And you know, sometimes you just *can't* cheer a person up. Sometimes, they just have to be miserable for a while and work through their heartache on their own terms.

Jesse, on the other hand, is taking a different approach: the I-want-to-get-the-hell-out-of-here-because-the-guilt-is-making-me-antsy approach.

Around noon, he asks, "Anyone wanna go to Starbucks? I could really go for a caffè mocha right now." He's so fidgety, I can't believe nobody's wondering what his problem is.

However, a trip to Starbucks would be the perfect opportunity to get him alone...

"I'll go," I offer.

Jesse tenses. I know that being alone with me is probably the last thing he wants right now, but that's just too bad. He's a big boy now. He can suck it up and deal with it.

"Okay," he agrees reluctantly. "Does anybody else want to go?"

For a moment, I'm afraid Sam might volunteer, but he's nodding off on the couch. He told me earlier that he didn't sleep very well. Cory kept him up talking about true love and fate until almost four in the morning.

"Nope. No one. Let's go," I announce, all but wrangling Jesse out the door.

"Way to be subtle," he gripes once we're alone and making our way down the hall.

"I'm sorry, but I have to talk to you and if you're going to keep avoiding me..." But the words die in my throat when the elevator door opens and a tall, tan, and impeccably dressed Tara Meeks steps out into the hallway. Well, *stomps* is more like it.

"Oh, shit," Jesse mutters under his breath.

"*You*," Tara hisses. At first, I think she's addressing Jesse. That is, until she marches right up to me, yanks my bag out of my hands and slams it down onto the floor, sending my lip gloss and loose change spilling out across the carpet. "How *dare* you?"

"Tara, listen to me, I don't - "

"You just couldn't let it go, could you? I warned you. I warned you, you little - "

"Hey!"

Sam and the others must have heard the commotion, because suddenly, they're all there in the hallway with us, eyeing Tara with looks ranging from shock to concern to outrage.

"What's going on?" Oliver asks.

"What are *you* doing here?" Joni snarls at Tara.

"I'm here to expose this little weasel for what she is. A lying, back-stabbing, self-righteous *shrew* who - "

"Hey!" Sam yells again, stepping between Tara and me. "No one, and I mean *no one*, talks to her like that."

And that's all it takes.

Tara's eyes narrow, and she tilts her head to the side, staring at Sam through luscious blonde bangs.

Then, to everyone's surprise, she laughs.

"Oh, my God. You're in love with her."

Sam stands his ground. If her accusation has caught him off guard, he doesn't show it. And he doesn't contradict her.

"How sweet. I bet she's in love with you, too, isn't she? Well, of course she is. Why else would you get matching tattoos?" she smirks.

"Matching tattoos?" Josh asks.

"Oh, you didn't know about that? He has a snowflake tattoo just like the stupid one she's got on her wrist." Upon seeing the confused looks on our faces, Tara explains, "Cory told me. He noticed it one night when Morneau went prancing around their room in his underwear. Of course, Cory didn't think anything of it because Mel and Sam are just *such good friends.*"

Dreadful anticipation is such a strange experience. I can feel my heart racing in my chest, I'm struggling to catch my breath, and my blood is buzzing throughout my entire body. Yet my face and my arms are freezing.

"Tara. It's not what you think." Oh, great. My voice just cracked. That's it. I'm dead.

"Isn't, Mel? Because I think it's *exactly* what I think. Which works out even better for me, because now I get to expose you for the lying little tramp you are in front of your friends *and* your boyfriend. Although, it seems that you've been keeping him a secret, too."

"Mel, *what* is she talking about?" Joni demands.

"I - I don't know..."

"Oh, yes you do, Mel. Why don't you tell them?" Tara asks sweetly. "Why don't you tell them that it was you who sold me out to the press? You are the one who's known about it for *months*, after all."

"What?" Oliver asks.

"Is that true, Mel?" Cory asks, speaking for the first time since Tara showed up.

"Of course it's not true," Sam insists. "Tara, I don't know who you think you're fooling, but you clearly don't know Mel. She would never keep something like that from us."

"You wanna bet, Lover Boy? Go ahead. Ask her yourself," Tara dares him.

Sam turns to look at me, certain to see the girl he's expecting to see, to hear the answer he's expecting to hear. I want to be that girl for him. I don't want him to know that he's wrong. But the tears welling in my eyes give me away, and in that moment, the only answer I can give him is barely a whisper.

"I'm sorry."

Now he's confused. They're all confused. But none of the other looks of hurt and betrayal break my heart the way that Sam's does. He's never looked at me like that before, like he doesn't know what to think. He's always looked at me like he knows exactly who I am, like he knows me better than I know myself. To see that distrust, that uncertainty in his eyes... I'm not sure I'll ever be able to erase that look from my conscience, or from my heart.

"I don't understand this. Mel, how could you have known?" Josh asks.

"I don't care how she knew. How could you not have told us? How could you not have told *me*?" Joni demands. She's furious. She has every right to be. But her anger cuts me just as deeply as Sam's sadness. In all the years we've been friends, Joni and I have never had a fight. Mild disagreements, sure. But never a fight.

"I - I didn't... I didn't want..." I have no idea how to explain myself without revealing the other truth. The one about Jesse being the man that Tara was seeing behind Cory's back. "I didn't want to burden anyone."

"You didn't want to *burden* us by doing the right thing?!" Joni rages. "Mel, how stupid can you be?"

That's it. There's only so much a person can take, and I've reached my limit. Humiliated, overwhelmed, and wracked with guilt, I bury my face in my hands and begin to sob.

157

"Hey, come on! She's not stupid!" To my surprise, the voice that jumps to my defense belongs not to Sam, or even to Oliver, but to Jesse. "And she doesn't deserve all this, either."

"Oh, really? You don't think she deserves this for being a rat-faced little snitch?" Tara hisses.

"No, I don't. Because she's not the one who snitched," Jesse retaliates. "I am."

"What?" Cory asks.

"Wait, Jess, you knew about it too?" Josh asks. "How?"

Tara, on the other hand, remains silent.

Jesse takes a deep breath.

"Because I'm the guy she was seeing."

CHAPTER 18

"If you want to walk on by me
Well I guess that's fine
And if you say I'm not the one
I guess I'll be alright
If you think we're better off
Without me kissing you goodnight
I guess I'll say that I'm okay
It wouldn't work out anyway
But please don't let me see you smile
My heart's not ready..."

Song: "Not Ready"
Artist: The Kind of September
From the Album: *17 Times Over*

There's an uncomfortable moment of absolute stillness. No one moves. No one seems to even breathe. Then, without a word, Cory storms off down the hall. Tara tries to follow him, but he brushes her off before he disappears into his room, slamming the door behind him.

"Cory! Cory, baby, please! Open the door! Let's talk about this!" Tara begs. But once she realizes that he's not going to answer her, she turns fiery eyes, not to Jesse, but to me.

"*This*," she hisses under her breath, "is all *your* fault!"

Then, with a sharp wail of anguish, she flees the scene and disappears back into the elevator. It's only then that all eyes turn to Jesse and me.

"What the hell just happened?" Josh asks.

Jesse is the one who answers.

"I don't even know where to begin," he confesses.

"You could start by telling us the truth," Oliver suggests, his tone hard and bitter. "The *whole* truth."

"I don't know what I was thinking," Jesse sighs. "When she and Cory first got together, I couldn't stand her. But the more she hung around, the more I found myself thinking about her. I began to see her the way Cory did: beautiful, fierce, independent, passionate. I never intended to act on it, but then we started talking. She would tease me, smile at me when no one was looking. It just... happened.

"When Melissa found out, we made her swear that she wouldn't tell anyone. She wanted to. She told us to end it. We didn't listen. I know I had no right to put that on her shoulders, but... I don't know. I thought it would end differently. I don't know why I thought that. It was stupid and selfish and... I'm sorry."

"Was it still going on?" Oliver asks.

"No. I ended it last month. I had thought, or at least hoped, that if Tara really cared about me, then she would have the courage to be honest with Cory, to maybe break it off with him so that we could be together. But she wasn't going to do that. It would be bad for her image. I finally figured out that she never really cared for either one of us. So I broke it off. And she did not take it well."

No, she didn't. I think back to our confrontation inside the supply closet.

"What happened?" Josh asks.

"It began with what I thought were empty threats. She was going to expose us. She was going to spread rumors about me to the media. But I didn't think she would, because that would be just as detrimental to her image as it was to mine. Then she began threatening the rest of you. So, I bought her silence, paid her to keep her mouth shut."

"What was she threatening?" Josh wonders.

"Lies. All lies. But they were horrible. False accusations of drug abuse, promiscuity. She said that she spent so much time with us that she could tell anyone that Sam liked to trash talk the fans or that Josh drank himself to sleep every night and they would believe her. Finally, I just couldn't take it anymore. I couldn't live with her blackmailing me. And I couldn't stand by and watch Cory fall in love with someone like her. He's a good guy. He's a good friend. But he couldn't see her for what she really was. He deserves better. He deserves a better woman than her and he definitely deserves a better friend than me."

"So why is Tara blaming Mel?" Oliver wants to know.

Jesse glances over at me. I don't know how to answer. So he answers sheepishly, "I kind of blamed the break-up on her."

"You what?" Sam finally speaks up.

"Melissa cornered me one day and... well... let's just say Tara isn't the only girl who knows how to make demands. Melissa's just a lot nicer about it."

Josh and Oliver seem to accept this. Maybe they've even forgiven me. But the way Joni is looking at me, it's like she's ready to spit poison.

"I can't believe it," she snaps. "I can't believe you didn't tell me."

Then, she shoves her way past me and barricades herself inside our room. I have a feeling I won't be welcome there for a while.

161

"I'm sorry," I whisper again, blinking back tears. It's only then that I finally look up at Sam. I've been too afraid to face him, terrified of what I might see in his eyes: anger, uncertainty, sadness, deception. But his eyes - those big, beautiful, expressive, blue eyes - are simply blank. "Sam... Please..."

"I um... I actually think I need to be alone, too," he mutters without looking me in the eye. "Excuse me."

Then he walks off down the hall and, following in Tara's footsteps, vanishes into the elevator, dragging my shattered heart behind him.

...

Since I really don't have anywhere else to go, Josh, Jesse, and Oliver let me go back with them to their room for the rest of the afternoon. None of us really know what to say. Jesse feels guilty. Oliver feels confused. Josh feels awkward. And me? I'm beginning to think Tara's right. This really is all my fault. Maybe if I'd never found out about her and Jesse in the first place, then none of this would have happened. Maybe it would have ended on its own. Maybe Tara would have ended up dumping *him*. Maybe, maybe, maybe...

What if this is the end? Of my friendship with Joni? Of my relationship with Sam? Of everything that we know and love and have worked so hard for?

No. No, that won't happen. The guys will work through it. Cory will forgive Jesse. He loves his band, his fans, his music, too much to let this come between them. We're all just emotional right now. And upset. And confused. We just need to sit back, to breathe, to let it all sink in. We'll get through this. We will.

"So Mel, is it true?" Josh asks, breaking the very uncomfortable silence.

"What?" I ask.

"You and Sam."

I pull my legs up to my chest, wrap my arms around them, and rest my head on my knees.

"It *was*," I reply. "Before this afternoon. But now..."

"He'll be okay," Jesse assures me. "Sam can't stay mad at anyone, especially you."

"But I've never kept anything from him before. Not anything like this. The way he looked at me... It was like he didn't even know who I was. Like the person he thought he knew all his life didn't exist..." I'm struggling to fight back a fresh wave of tears.

"Personally, I can't believe the two of you kept *this* from us," Josh remarks. "I mean, we all kind of thought it would happen eventually. I just really didn't think that we were a group that kept secrets from each other."

"Every group has their secrets," Oliver murmurs.

He's right. I'm *still* keeping his secret crush on Joni. And I'm keeping her secret relationship with Chris. What's next? A secret lovechild? A secret wedding in Vegas? For better or for worse, secrets are everywhere, and they don't like to stay hidden.

"We were going to tell you," I say. "But then all of this happened. Cory was so sad. It just didn't feel like the right time. Now I'm afraid I've ruined everything."

"Stop blaming yourself. You didn't do anything," Jesse assures me.

"I know," I sigh. "And that's exactly why I *do* blame myself."

Just then, someone knocks on the door. Josh goes to open it. It's Sam.

For the first time in my life, my heart pounds not with delight, but with a terrible sense of fear and anxiety, at the sight of his handsome face.

"Hey," he mutters, brushing his hair back away from his face before shoving both hands inside his pockets. It's strange to see him so sheepish, so unsure. I don't know what it means. "Is she here?"

"Yeah," Josh steps aside, inviting Sam into the room.

"Hi." I stand to greet him, my knees trembling.

163

"Hi," he echoes. "Can we talk? Just you and me?"

I nod, afraid that if I open my mouth to speak, I'll start to cry.

Together, we step out onto the balcony. By now, the sun has begun to set. It's a deep, vibrant sundown that sets the sky ablaze with oranges and magentas and even a dash of violet; a beautiful end to a rather ugly day.

"Mel, I just wanted to say..." Sam begins. "I just wanted to say that I'm sorry for the way I acted this afternoon."

"Sam, you don't have to apologize." I'm the one who should be sorry, not him.

"Well, I feel like a jerk for walking off like that. For leaving you when I knew that you were hurting."

"You were hurting too. I could see that," I confess. "And it kills me to know that I'm the cause of it." Tears are beginning to roll down my cheeks again. I don't bother trying to stop them.

"No, Mel, it wasn't you. I just... I guess I'm just more confused than anything. I don't understand why you didn't tell me."

I shake my head.

"There were so many times I almost told you. I wanted to. Believe me, Sam, I wanted to tell you more than anything. But every time I got close, I would think about the tour and how excited you are and how much you love your music and your band... I didn't want you to see Jesse the way that I saw him. And I didn't want to put you in the position to have to betray one of your friends. I couldn't burden you with that. I didn't want to ruin what was supposed to be the best year of your life. And I don't know if I made the right decision. I probably didn't. And I'm sorry, Sam. I'm so, so sorry."

Without skipping a beat, Sam pulls me into his arms and holds me while I cry. I bury my face in his shoulder, my heart heavy with guilt and relief and so much love that it begins to ache.

164

"I was afraid that you didn't trust me," Sam murmurs into my hair.

"What?" I pull back and stare up at him. I don't believe what I'm hearing.

"It's silly, I know. But I thought that maybe you didn't think I could handle it, or that I would try and force you into something that you weren't comfortable with."

"Sam, no. I trust you with everything. I trust you with my whole life. I just wanted you to be happy. That's all I've ever wanted."

Uncharacteristically somber, Sam takes my face in his hands and wipes my tears away with his thumbs. "You can't protect me from everything, Mel. I know how hard that is to accept. I'm finally beginning to accept that I can't protect *you* from everything. If I could, none of this would have happened. I just hope you know that you can always come to me, no matter what. I love you. Your burdens are my burdens."

"I love you, too," I whimper and wrap my arms back around his shoulders.

"You know, speaking of which, I guess *our* secret is out now," Sam grins down at me.

"Looks like it," I reply, drying the remainder of my tears with the back of my sleeve. "I kind of wish it had come out under different circumstances..."

Sam chuckles. "Well, to be fair, I don't think anyone was really surprised."

"They weren't," I assure him. "Maybe Joni was."

Saying her name out loud was a mistake. A new wave of gut-wrenching remorse washes over me as I remember the look in her eyes earlier this afternoon. If I weren't such a coward, I would go check on her, see if she's okay. But I don't know if I can face her. Not yet.

As if he can actually hear what I'm thinking, Sam looks down at me and says, "Hey, she's going to be okay. She's just upset right now. But she knows this wasn't you."

"I hope so." I hope Cory knows it, too. "Have you talked to Cory at all?"

"No. I thought it best just to give him some time to absorb everything. Work through it."

"You're probably right," I sigh. "I just hope that he'll be able to forgive Jesse."

This is normally the point in the conversation where Sam jumps in and assures me, *"Of course he'll be able to forgive Jesse! They're best friends! No woman could ever come between them!"* Sam is the optimist, the one who can always see the bright side of any situation. It's one of the many things that makes him so wonderful.

But he says nothing of the sort. In fact, he doesn't say anything at all. And his silence speaks volumes. As much as he'd like to, he doesn't believe that Cory will forgive Jesse. He doesn't believe this is something they can overcome. And if that all turns out to be true, if this rift between Cory and Jesse can't be mended, it might mean more than the end of their friendship.

It might mean the end of The Kind of September.

CHAPTER 19

"This will be the last time
Tonight, it all shall end
Three valiant steps, two beating hearts,
One chance to live again
I said that I'm your rebel
You said that you're my friend
I think I'm gonna take this down
There's no turning back now..."

Song: "Rebel"
Artist: Morning Muses
From the Album: *Nightfall*

It's been almost twenty hours since any of us have seen or heard from Cory. Even Sam. He and I camped out in the rest of the guys' room last night, so neither of us slept very well. I don't think anyone else did, either. And of course, we have to be awake bright and early to film one last promotional video for the tour. In fact, we should be on our way to the studio now, but we're still waiting on Cory. That's just not like him.

"Do you think one of us should go check on him?" Jesse asks.

"Well, I don't think it should be you," Josh remarks. Of all the guys, I actually think he's the one having the hardest time processing Tara and Jesse's affair. Although Josh has a reputation for being the loud, silly, outlandish one, in many ways, I think he's also the most innocent. Life is just so good, so simple for him. I don't think he really understands what happened, or how Jesse could do such a thing to his friend. Then again, I'm not sure any of us do.

"I wasn't offering," Jesse murmurs.

"I'll go," Sam volunteers.

"What about Joni?" Oliver asks once Sam is out of the room.

"You know her. She's probably already there," Jesse states.

"You still haven't heard from her, Mel?" Oliver asks.

I shake my head. Admitting that my best friend isn't speaking to me makes me feel even more like a villain than I already do. I haven't told the guys, but I'm dreading seeing her this morning. It's not that I can't handle being yelled at, or that I'm afraid of confrontation, though I'm not a fan of either. It's that I know that whatever she says to me is going to be true. And as difficult as it is to accept ourselves as we are, sometimes it's even more difficult to come face to face with the way others see us.

"I hope she's okay," Oliver continues.

"She's fine. She's just really pissed off," Josh huffs. He sounds extremely tired of talking about Joni. And Cory. And everything. I can't say I blame him.

"Still, I think I might send her a message. Make sure everything is alright," Oliver announces and reaches into his pocket for his phone just as my own phone begins to chime.

It's a text message from Sam.

Need help. Hurry.

168

Panicking, I sprint out of the guys' room, down the hall to Cory and Sam's room. The door is already open, so I let myself in. At first glance, the room is totally empty and for a moment, I wonder if I've accidentally barged into the wrong one. Then I hear a most unpleasant noise: sputtering, gagging, coughing.

"It's okay, buddy. It's okay. Just get it up," Sam's voice echoes from inside the bathroom.

I take a cautious step towards the door and ease it open to reveal Cory - ghastly, white, and very, very sick - collapsed in front of the toilet. Sam is standing over him, patting his back and looking pretty miserable himself.

"Cory?" I try to speak gently. I remember the last time I was sick to my stomach, loud voices somehow made me feel even queasier. Of course, I don't think this is a common stomach bug. This is something a little more self-inflicted.

Cory doesn't look up at me, but Sam does.

"Looks like we've got ourselves something of a hangover," he comments.

Well, if this just isn't the absolute last thing we need. I feel bad for Cory. I really do. Life dealt him a pretty crappy hand last night. But getting himself wasted when he knows that he has to be at a video shoot? There are so many better ways to handle a broken heart than getting dead drunk alone in a hotel room. Join a dating site. Write a song. Just stay away from the alcohol, especially if your name is Cory Foreman and you *know* that you're a lightweight! Seriously, the first time he ever got drunk, he stripped down to his boxer shorts and danced around on a coffee table. Now granted, this was in high school, so he may have built up his tolerance a *little*, but clearly not by very much! *What* made him think he could handle this?

"Okay. What do you need me to do?" I ask.

"Find water. Water and Advil. If you need to call room service, that's fine," Sam instructs.

169

"Actually, I think we have some Advil in our room." In fact, I know we do. Joni and I always have a bottle on hand for one reason or another.

"Perfect."

By the time I return with Advil and three bottles of water, Cory is back in bed while Sam paces back and forth across the room, talking to someone on the phone.

"Is there any way we can postpone? I know it's unprofessional but Cory... he's just really sick. He can barely stand up. There's no way he's going to be able to go through with this.... No, I know. Trust me, I get it, it's just that... Okay... Yeah. I heard you the first time... Okay."

Finally, Sam hangs up the phone, tosses it onto his bed, and rubs his face in his hands.

"What's going on?" I wonder.

"Joni says we're not rescheduling the shoot," he mutters. "She thinks it would be unprofessional and she can't believe I would even ask such a careless question."

I can't help but think it might be equally unprofessional to show up haggard and hungover, but I don't want to say anything on the off chance that Cory might still be conscious. So instead, I argue, "She doesn't even care that it's her brother who's sick?"

"If anything, that's making her less sympathetic."

"So, what do we do? Drag Cory down to the vans?"

"That or wheel him out on a stretcher," Sam remarks, resting his hands on his hips and staring down at his pale, clammy roommate.

"Well, maybe once we get some water and Advil in him, he'll feel a little better," I suggest.

"Yeah. If nothing else, we at least need to get him hydrated," Sam agrees.

It takes some coaxing, but Cory finally opens his eyes and even manages to sit up and drink some water. He looks awful. His hair is a mess, his skin is completely white, almost a pale green, and his eyes are dark and sunken in. He kind of

170

looks like a vampire but without the sex appeal. He's also unshaven and he reeks of puke and liquor. This is not a guy ready to film a promotional video for a world tour.

Sam seems to feel the same way.

"Okay, Mel, run back down to the others' room. Tell them to go on without us. We'll take the second van and meet them there."

"Right."

...

By the time Sam, Cory, and I arrive at the studio, the rest of the guys are already in the middle of hair and make-up. Hopefully, Tiffany, the guys' primary stylist, is prepared to work a few miracles on Cory. He hasn't said a whole lot since Sam got him up and moving, but at least he's able to stand and walk on his own. I think that's a good sign.

Joni appears as Sam and Cory take their seats in front of the vanity mirrors, but she acts as though she doesn't even see me. She simply stares down at her clipboard and passes a few notes on to the guys.

Once the guys line up for the shoot itself, it becomes painstakingly clear that none of them are in the mood to film this video. Sam is stressed, Jesse is fidgety, Josh is bitter, Oliver is at his wit's end, and Cory... well, he looks like a zombie. He's acting like it, too. His eyes are drooping, he keeps swaying on the spot, and any noise louder than a whisper makes him wince.

What is happening to us? This isn't how it used to be, how it should be. We should all be thrilled to be here. The new tour begins in less than two weeks! The guys have worked so hard on this new album, and they're so proud of it. It's by far their best one to date. But instead of celebrating the music and enjoying the excitement and anticipation of yet another amazing adventure, they're here in the midst of heartbreak and scandal and drunken nights that should never have even taken place. This isn't the band that I know, despite how the media tries to portray them. They're not drunks.

They're not cheaters. They're brothers. They care about each other. They have fun together. How could this have happened?

"Hi. We're The Kind of September," Sam recites his line for the camera. "We're happy that you could join us for this, our third world tour."

"We're excited to visit old friends in some of our very favorite cities," Josh says.

"And to make... Um... And meet... New friends..." Cory stammers, pressing the heel of his hand to his forehead.

"Cut!" Sarah, the director, yells. "Let's try that again. From the top!"

Cory fumbles the line again. And again.

"Are you sure you're feeling up to this, Cory?" Josh asks.

"I'm fine. I just... need a minute," Cory mumbles.

"You know, it's okay if you're not," Oliver tells him. "We know it's been hard - "

"I said I'm fine!" Cory snaps.

Everyone is startled by his sudden outburst. Oliver and Sam flinch. Josh actually takes a step back, away from him. Jesse, on the other hand, just stares down at the floor.

"Is everything okay with them?" Sarah asks me, her brown eyes full of concern behind her trendy black glasses. This is the first time we've ever worked with her, and I'm terribly afraid we're not making a very good impression.

"Um, yeah. Just a bit tired, is all," I assure her.

"Is Cory feeling alright?"

"I think he's fighting off something." I've been in this industry long enough to know that you never, ever, ever badmouth your clients, especially your famous clients, and that's technically what the guys are to me. Of course, they're my best friends first. But they've also hired me to do a job for them. In this setting, I'm not their pal, Mel. I'm their design and photography intern, Melissa Parker.

"Oh, that's unfortunate," Sarah remarks. Then, she addresses the guys, "You know, if we need to, we can reassign some of the lines. Jesse, do you think you can - "

"No!" Cory interjects.

Sarah looks startled.

"I'm sorry?" she asks.

"No. Jesse is not going to cover for me. *Jesse* has already done enough." Cory spits.

Clearly shaken, Sarah looks back at me, but I'm afraid I'm feeling just as helpless as she is. I've never seen Cory like this. He's always so calm, so in-control. He's usually the one the rest of us look to for a sense of reason and maturity.

"Cory... I'm sorry, man... If I could take it all back, I would." Jesse's apology is utterly sincere, but I think we all know that it's too little, too late.

"You're *sorry*? Well, great, Jesse! That makes everything *all better*!" Cory lashes out.

It's only then, in the middle of Cory's very public breakdown, that Joni finally decides to show up.

"Stop it! Stop it, both of you!" she scolds them.

"I haven't done *anything*! I am the victim here!" Cory hollers at his sister.

"Be that as it may, you are still a member of this group and you have a job to do. This is neither the time nor place - "

"I don't believe this! Are you actually taking his side?" Cory asks.

"Of course not!" Joni exclaims, her eyebrows fixed and furrowed as though the very idea appalls her.

"Cory, there are no sides." Sam tries to reason with him, but it does him no good.

"Oh, sure, you *would* say that. After all, you're the one sneaking around with the girl who knew everything and *didn't say a word*," Cory hisses in Sam's face. "I'm surprised she didn't tell *you*. Or maybe she did and you were too busy dragging her to bed to listen - "

It takes the combined efforts of Jesse, Josh, and Oliver to keep Sam from lunging at Cory, who takes a stumbling step backwards, but smirks when he sees how effective his words were.

"Sam, Sam, it's okay!" I step in, trying to calm him down.

"No, it's *not* okay!" Sam yells. Then, he turns his attention to Cory. "Don't you ever, *ever* say anything like that about her again! Do you hear me?"

Cory just scoffs it off.

Even though I know he's hurting and that he (hopefully) doesn't mean anything he says, Cory's disdain hurts me more than I care to admit. He's one of my oldest friends. We grew up together. And to hear him talk about me in such a degrading and spiteful way is like a punch in the stomach.

"Cory, what has gotten into you?" Oliver demands. "Look, I know how you must be feeling, but - "

"You know how I must be feeling?" Cory cries, exasperated, at his friend. "You have no *idea* how I'm feeling, Oliver! You've never been in love! Hell, have you ever even held hands with a woman?"

"Cory, stop it! Come on, man. Please!" Jesse begs. "You can be mad at me all you want, but don't take it out on the rest of the group. I'm the one whose ass you want to kick. If it would make you feel better, go for it. Just leave them out of it!"

"Hey, you are the *last* person I want to be taking advice from right now!"

By now, everyone is shouting to be heard. Oliver and Josh have formed a human barricade in between Cory and Jesse while I keep a tight hold on Sam's arm.

"*Alright! That's enough!*" Joni screams. The fighting subsides momentarily.

It's in that moment of calm and silence that I realize every eye in the studio is locked on us. A few onlookers have their smart phones out, recording the entire incident.

No, no, no.

"You're right, Jo. That is enough," Cory mutters, glaring at his bandmates with what I can only describe as contempt. "I'm done."

A heavy stillness falls upon the room and everyone standing around seems to be holding their breath.

"What do you mean?" Josh asks, his voice small and timid for quite possibly the first time in his life. "Cory, what do you mean, you're done?"

"I'm not doing this anymore. I can't. I can't be around any of you. And I especially can't be around *him*." He indicates Jesse.

"But... But what about the tour?" Oliver wants to know.

"You can go on tour without me. I won't be missed," Cory mutters bitterly. "From this moment on, I am no longer a part of The Kind of September."

CHAPTER 20

"I've tried to run and hide
From the rain that's falling down
But she kicked off her shoes
And cast them to the ground
'Oh won't you come and dance with me?'
She bade me with a smile
How could I resist her?
How could I resist her?
I guess the real world
Will just have to wait a while..."

Song: "Rain"
Artist: The Kind of September
From the Album: *Meet Me on the Midway*

Stormy September: Cory Foreman QUITS The Band!

Could this be the end of the world's most popular boy band? *According to a number of eyewitness accounts, Cory Foreman lashed out at his friend and fellow band member, Jesse Scott, after reports of a cheating scandal involving Foreman's girlfriend, Tara Meeks, surfaced a few days ago. Several sources have now* confirmed that Scott was, in fact, the other man in Miss Meeks' now very public life.

After confronting both Scott and Meeks about the affair, Foreman announced his resignation from The Kind of September, who recently released their third album, Meet Me on the Midway, and are in the midst of preparing for their third world tour. Although none of Foreman's bandmates have spoken publicly about his departure, sources assure us that Jesse Scott, along with Oliver Berkley, Josh Cahill, and fan favorite, Sam Morneau, have no plans to cancel or postpone their upcoming tour.

Representatives for Cory Foreman and Tara Meeks both declined to comment.

Well, the good news, if there is any, is that this isn't the first time a story like this has popped up in the tabloids.

The bad news is that this time, it just so happens to be true. And the fans are starting to panic. When the story first broke, I think they were in denial. And they had every reason to be. It seems like every other week, a gossip column is claiming that this time, it really *is* the end of The Kind of September.

Unfortunately for Jesse, while the fans might not be convinced that Cory is actually leaving the band, the media has most of them believing that he was the one seeing Tara behind Cory's back. And most of them are *not* okay with that.

Even though I'm heartbroken for @CoryTKOS, I'm even more heartbroken that @JScottTKOS would betray him like this. I thought #TKOS was a family.

I just want to know HOW intoxicated Jesse had to be to hook up with Tara. Like, have you not seen how awful she is?! #GoHomeJesseYoureDrunk

Looking at pictures of Cory and Jesse throughout the years and sobbing into a bowl of cold pasta. #SupportCory

A very loyal few, however, are flat out refusing to believe the reports.

Seriously, there is NO way Jesse was the one Tara was cheating with. That ISN'T the Jesse we know! #StopTheLies

177

If all these rumors about @JScottTKOS and @ItsTaraMeeks turn out to be true, I will lose faith in everything.

DON'T WORRY JESSE. WE BELIEVE IN YOU. #JesseIsMyWorld #JesseGirlForever

As for the rumor that Cory has left the band, most fans aren't even acknowledging it. And if they are, they certainly aren't accepting it.

Come on. HOW many times have we heard that one of the guys is leaving? #TKOS

I refuse to believe ANYTHING until Cory himself announces that he's leaving.

If Cory quits, my life will be over. #PleaseStayCory #SupportCory

As several fans have pointed out, no one has made any official statements about Cory leaving the band. He still has a contract, after all, and there are things he's going to need to work out before any final decisions can be made. The rest of the guys are getting pretty anxious. I know how they feel. I like to know what's going to happen. All this uncertainty... it's like being in Limbo. Although I think we're all pretty certain of how it's going to play out.

That just leaves the Jesse and Tara rumors. The guys have decided not to address them at all, and it doesn't seem that Tara cares to confirm them either. We haven't heard a word from her since our confrontation in the hallway two days ago. It might be too much to hope that she may be gone for good, but there's no harm in keeping our fingers crossed.

Joni still isn't talking to me. In fact, she got herself her own room for the remainder of our time here at the hotel. After she moved out, I broke down crying in Sam's arms. He didn't really have any advice or words of comfort to offer, but he was there for me, and he stayed with me all night. That was enough.

Even so, I can't help but wonder if things may have been different if I had been honest up front, if I had gone to Cory, or at least Sam or Joni, the second I found out about

178

Jesse and Tara. It may not have spared Cory the heartbreak, and I would have been betraying Jesse in the process, but at least my friendship with Joni would still be intact.

Sam has tried to remind me that there was no easy way out of this. There wasn't a decision that I could have made that wouldn't have left someone feeling hurt.

I think I'm dwelling on this too much. After all, what's done is done and nothing I say or do can rewrite the past. But the thing is if Cory does leave, if this really is the end of The Kind of September, then it's all my fault. If that happens, if everything that has come to mean so much to so many people falls apart because of me, I don't know how I'll be able to live with myself. And what about Sam? He and the rest of the guys have worked so hard for their music. They deserve everything in the world. And here it is, crumbling around us and there's not a thing any of us can do to stop it.

I keep thinking that any second now, I'm going to wake up and this will all turn out to just be a terrible dream. The guys will all be smiling and laughing and talking about how great the tour is going to be. Joni will be complaining to me about one thing or another, probably something that Cory did or said. And I'll be making plans for a secret date with Sam.

I guess it's a good thing that we don't have to sneak around anymore, but honestly, neither of us has been feeling very romantic these last couple of days. We still love each other, but it's hard to enjoy a relationship, or anything really, when everyone around you, especially everyone you care about, is hurting so badly.

Speaking of relationships, I can't help but wonder if Joni has told Chris about all of this, or if she'll keep seeing him after her brother quits the band.

Oh my God. Her brother is quitting the band. What does that mean for her? Will she leave us too? I can't imagine she would want to stay without Cory. What will we do without them?

Sam just received this text from Josh: **Hey, come down to our room. Cory wants to talk to us.**

We both look at each other.

"Well," Sam sighs. "I guess this is it."

...

Once we've all gathered, Joni included, Cory stands up and clears his throat.

"I've been doing some thinking," he announces. "After talking it over with Joni and with management, going over the contract and everything, I've decided it wouldn't be fair to you and it wouldn't be fair to the fans to leave - "

"Yes!" Josh exclaims.

" - yet," Cory finishes.

"Yet?" Sam asks.

"You mean you're still quitting?" Oliver asks.

"Yes, but not until after the tour," Cory answers.

"Cory, then what's the point?" Josh asks. "If you're going to stay for the tour, then just stay!"

"Or at least don't make any hasty decisions," Jesse advises.

But it is still way too soon for Cory to even consider listening to Jesse.

"*Hasty* decisions? This is the biggest decision I've ever made in my life. This is probably the biggest decision I *will* ever make. Do you know how much I'm giving up? This is my life. The music, the fans... But I can't do it anymore."

"Because of me?" Jesse demands.

"Yes, because of you! And because of the rumors and the secrets. Because of the media running and ruining every aspect of our lives. Because everything I thought we were as a group, as a team, as friends... it all turned out to be a lie. Let's face it, none of us are the guys that the fans see when we step out on stage. But somewhere along the line, I think we all deluded ourselves into believing that we were, and that life is just as bright and exhilarating and perfect as it is

180

whenever we perform. But it's not. We're not. And I'm finally beginning to see that."

"So, what, your solution is to just walk away?" Jesse asks. "I made a mistake, Cory! I made a mistake and I'm sorry. But everything you just talked about, this group, this music, these are all *good* things! And no, we're not perfect. I know we're not perfect. But I think what we have here is as close to perfect as it's ever going to get!"

Cory closes his eyes and takes a few deep breaths before he opens them again.

"Jesse, I don't want to fight with you."

"Good! I don't want to fight with you either!"

"Then *stop* talking," Cory hisses. "Look, you might not *get* this, considering the way you go through women, but being with Tara meant something to me. It was special. And you took her without a second thought. Like she was just another conquest."

"You know, Cory, not that I'm condoning what Jesse did by any means, but it does take two to Tango," Josh remarks. "From what Jesse's told us, she didn't try to stop him. In fact, it sounds to me like she may have encouraged him."

"No. That isn't true," Cory snaps. "Tara wouldn't have done that to me. If she did, it's because *he* seduced her!"

"Cory," Sam finally speaks up. "I'm not trying to defend anyone or to make you feel worse than you already do, but don't you think that if Tara had really cared about you, she wouldn't have even considered being with Jesse?"

"No, stop it!" Cory cries, holding his hands up in the air. "I'm done, okay? I'm done talking about this. It's painful and it's humiliating and I'm just done. I said what I came in here to say. I'll stay until the end of the tour. After that, I'm gone."

"And I think it goes without saying that I'll be leaving as well," Joni announces.

181

"But Jo..." I don't know what I think I can say that would make her change her mind, but the words die in my throat anyway as I struggle not to start crying. Again.

Joni glances over at me, a nasty scowl on her pretty face, and then turns away without a word. Sam must have seen, because he wraps an arm around my shoulders and pulls me gently against his chest.

After Cory and Joni excuse themselves, Josh asks, "So what's going to happen to the rest of us?"

No one seems to have an answer for him.

"I guess that's just something we're going to have to figure out for ourselves," Sam finally replies.

"Or it might be something that the fans decide for us," Oliver murmurs.

"I'm sorry, guys," Jesse apologizes yet again. "This is all my fault."

"Do me a favor, Jess, and just stop with the pity party, okay?" Josh asks. "You screwed up. Great. We get it. But we need to focus on the future now. And salvaging whatever we can of this group."

"Josh is right," Sam says. "Even if it's just one day at a time. We concentrate on the tour. The tour, the music, and the fans."

"Agreed," Oliver pipes up.

"Agreed," Josh echoes.

All eyes turn toward Jesse.

"Agreed."

CHAPTER 21

"I think I'll change my name
I think I'll do things right
I think I'll pack my bags
And run away tonight
So take me to that highway
Take me to that shore
Take me to those mountains
I'm needing something more
I'll change my name..."

Song: "Change My Name"
Artist: Chloe Conley
From the Album: *Chloe*

The news about Cory officially broke last night. I haven't had the heart to check what the media and the fans are saying, but from what the guys have told me, the reactions range from *"I'll never be able to listen to Cory's solos without crying"* to *"This is the worst thing that could ever happen to me."*

None of us, however, have been able to avoid the seemingly endless stream of text messages, calls, and emails pouring in from family members, close friends, and even acquaintances whose names I would have forgotten were they not stored safely in the SD card of my smart phone.

Chloe is one of the firsts to text me.

Mel, is it true? Is Cory really quitting?

Yes. After the tour. I reply.

Oh my God! I just can't believe it. How are the rest of the guys? she asks.

They're doing okay. I don't think it's really sunk in yet.

The next person to message me is my sister.

Mel PLEASE tell me that Cory isn't leaving the band!

And then Kendra.

Is Cory okay? A girl in my Calc class just told me he's quitting TKOS!

And of course, my mother.

If Cory is leaving, does that mean Joni is as well? Because I don't know how I feel about you being the only girl out there with all those boys. I know they're your friends, but at their age and with all their antics, I just don't know if you should be alone with them. Maybe I should call Mrs. Foreman. Do you think Joni would consider staying even if Cory isn't around? I just can't believe this is happening. Also, I hope you remembered to pack your winter coat. It's still pretty chilly in most parts of the country.

I have no idea how to respond to all of that, particularly the part about Joni. How am I supposed to tell my frantic, overprotective mother that not only is Joni not staying, she's also no longer speaking to me because this whole mess is kind-of-sort-of-partially my fault? And oh yeah, by the way, I'm totally dating one of "those boys." You know, the ones she doesn't want me to be alone with without Joni there to chaperone.

It kills me to even think it, but if it were up to my mother, this would be my last tour with the guys too. The fact that I am well over the age of eighteen and no longer legally bound to do what she tells me means absolutely nothing to her. I know it's only because she loves me and wants what's best for me, but she knows how much I love working with them. She knows how much I love *them*. I think all the rumors really get to her, and even though, deep down, she knows most of them aren't true, she scared that this world that we're in is toxic. And yeah, I guess parts of it are. But for the most part, it's a good environment with good people.

If nothing else, it's a heck of an adventure.

Meanwhile, the guys are being flooded with well wishes, condolences, and literally thousands of questions, most of which have no answer. No good answer, anyway, and certainly not the answers that the fans want to hear.

To many, Cory's departure is confirmation that Tara did, in fact, have an affair with Jesse, and several of them have turned on him. But overall, they still refuse to abandon the rest of the group, especially since Sam, Josh, and Oliver need their love and support now more than ever. And Cory. Poor, forsaken Cory. If he were a politician, his approval ratings would be skyrocketing. Suddenly, everyone loves him. He's everyone's favorite member. And I think it might be making him feel a little better. Not that he's said anything to me, or the rest of the group for that matter. For the most part, he's kept to himself. But he doesn't seem as miserable as he did yesterday. Maybe he feels relieved that everything is out in the open about his impending departure.

I just want him to be okay. I want all of us to be okay.

Jesse has been pretty quiet these last few days as well. Although I wasn't present for it, Sam told me that he, Oliver, and Josh had a long talk with Jesse about what he did. They basically told him that they were disappointed in him, Josh even confessed to being pissed off, but they still wanted him to be a part of the group. They're not going to let this get in the way of their friendship. Granted, they might have been singing a different tune if Jesse had been sneaking around with one of *their* girlfriends, but I hope Sam at least knows

185

that I care far too much about him to even give other guys a second look.

Except maybe that one Irish singer-songwriter. But you know, I'd never actually do anything with him. He's just very easy on the eyes.

...

With our remaining days in Los Angeles numbered, I've been trying my best to get organized, to get all my laundry done, and to make sure I don't forget anything when we leave the hotel. However, since Sam has all but moved into my room with me, I find my will power and determination beginning to waver. Not because I'm so in love that his mere presence is a distraction (though he *can* be very distracting, and he knows it too) but because he is so messy that it doesn't matter *how* tidy I am. His spectacular filth is simply more powerful than my cleaning prowess.

Case in point: I just found his toothbrush in a sock. I have no idea how that happened, but I make a mental note to run down to the lobby to buy him a new one just as soon as I've found my wallet, which, last time I checked was on my nightstand but has since been displaced by two empty potato chip bags and a half-full liter of soda.

And this isn't even half as bad as it will be on the tour bus.

You know, the funny thing is I'm actually *not* a neat freak. It's just that anyone in the world would seem like one compared to Samuel Spencer Morneau -

"Mel!"

- who just happened to burst through the door with a panic-stricken look on his handsome face.

That can't be good.

"What's going on?" I ask him.

Instead of answering, he hands me his smart phone. At first, I'm not sure what I'm looking at. It's a photograph, but it's blurred, sort of like a screen shot of a video, or maybe an image off of a security camera.

Security camera.

All of a sudden, something clicks and I realize that I'm staring at a picture of a couple embracing in a hotel hallway. More specifically *our* hotel hallway.

And the young man in the picture is Sam.

And the girl that he's kissing is me.

There's an article accompanying the picture.

Sam and Melissa: Exposed!

Does the drama never end? Amidst widespread rumors of infidelity, scandal, and an impending break-up, new reports are surfacing that Sam Morneau, easily the most notorious face in The Kind of September, has a new love in the form of an old friend.

Melissa Parker, 21, is well known for being a longtime supporter of the band, often seen traveling with them and credited for a number of photographs that appear on their website. But according to an insider source, the soft-spoken brunette has recently added the occupation 'girlfriend' to her already enviable TKOS resume.

The source went on to claim that Morneau and Parker have been secretly dating for months, often spending hours of their time together in their respective hotel rooms. The two most recently celebrated Valentine's Day in an as of yet undisclosed location.

This isn't the first time Parker has been linked to a member of the popular boy band. She is rumored to have dated Oliver Berkley for an extended period of time before engaging in a brief fling with Jesse Scott. Perhaps third time's a charm?

I can't think. I'm not sure I even remember how to breathe.

"Is this... Um... What... Is this... I..." Yeah, that's definitely not a sentence.

It was Tara. It had to be Tara. I don't know how, but I know that she's behind this. She's the only one who *could* be behind it. She's definitely the only one who would do something like this.

But *why*? Why is she doing this? I'm not the one who leaked her cheating scandal! Is this some sort of sick revenge?

187

For what? Telling Jesse to break up with her? Or is she simply trying to sabotage what remains of The Kind of September?

This isn't happening. This can't be happening.

"It gets worse," Sam warns me.

"Worse?!" I squeak. "How could it get worse?"

He opens his Twitter app. The phrase *Sam and Mel* is first on the list of worldwide trending topics. *#TKOS* and *#Meliver* are third and seventh.

Are those pictures of Sam and Mel real?! Like are they REAL REAL?!!!?!??

Pictures of Sam and Mel look photoshopped. This is just a publicity stunt to distract us from all the Cory and Jesse drama. #TKOS #Stop

Sam is dating Melissa Parker?! What about #Meliver?

So do all the #TKOS guys share girls or what? #SamAndMel #OliverAndMel #CoryAndTara #JesseAndTara #JoshAndPizza

If Sam has a girlfriend I actually do not know what I am going to do with my life. #Sobbing

UNTIL SAM CONFIRMS IT I AM NOT BELIEVING ANYTHING. MEL IS NOT DATING SAM. SHE IS WITH OLIVER.

Fairly certain the entire #TKOS fandom just suffered a crippling mental and emotional breakdown.

That's funny. I think I'm about to suffer a crippling mental and emotional breakdown myself.

"Oh my God." I take several deep breaths in and out. "Oh my God. Okay. What do we do?"

"Whatever you tell me," Sam says, tossing his smart phone aside and onto my bed. "If you want me to deny it, claim that it's a fake, then I will." Then he takes my hands and looks me in the eye. "This doesn't have to be your life. Not yet."

I know that he means well, that he's only trying to protect me. But it seems the more we try to hide, the more trouble we find ourselves in. And that's what Tara wants.

She sold us out to the press for the sole purpose of dragging us down and throwing us off guard. I'm not about to give her that satisfaction.

"You're right," I tell him. "It doesn't have to be my life. You could deny everything and this would all go away. But when the day comes that we finally do tell everyone, then all your fans are going to know that we lied to them initially. And I'm not going to make you do that. I'm not going to let them think badly of you."

As I speak the words, Sam pulls me into his arms and presses his lips to my forehead.

"I love you, Mel."

"I love you, too," I murmur into his neck. Then I pull back and look up to meet his eye. "Let's tell them."

"Are you sure?" he asks.

"Sam, I've always known that being with you... that it would never be a normal relationship. That we can't just go out and hold hands on a Friday night without a million cameras going off or without someone stopping you and asking for your autograph. I know that there will be rumors and criticism and negativity, but like I said to you that night back in November, you're worth it. If that's the price I have to pay to love you, to spend my life with you, then so be it."

Sam takes my face in his hands and kisses me lightly on the lips.

"What did I do to deserve you?" he whispers.

I kiss him in response. Then I pick up his phone and hold it out to him. He takes it and begins to type out a new message, but he quickly deletes it.

"What's wrong?" I ask.

"This just sounds too formal. It makes it seem like we just got caught."

"Well, we kind of did," I remind him.

"I know. But I don't want whoever did this thinking that they got the better of us," he tells me. He stops to think for a moment. All of a sudden, his eyes light up. "I've got it."

189

Then he stretches his arm up, holding his phone as far away his face as possible. "You wouldn't be willing to take a selfie with me, would you?"

I see where he's going with this.

"I'd be delighted to."

Sam takes two pictures of us: one of us smiling side by side, and one of him kissing me on the lips. We've never taken a picture like that before, but I'm not going to lie, I kind of like it.

"What's the caption going to be?" I ask Sam as he prepares to send both pictures out into the Twitter universe.

He holds up his phone so that I can read what he wrote.

I love this girl.

"Plain and simple." He grins and my heart melts.

"It's perfect," I tell him.

"Okay." His thumb hovers over the **Send Tweet** button on his smart phone screen. "See you on the other side, Miss Parker."

I take his free hand and give him one last swift kiss on the cheek.

"I'm ready when you are."

ACKNOWLEDGEMENTS

I'm afraid all of my acknowledgements sections are becoming painstakingly similar. I've been trying to come up with ways to make them a little more entertaining. I considered maybe writing a poem, but then I remembered that I'm terrible at poetry. Those lyrics at the beginning of each chapter are about all I can come up with, and half of those aren't even mine!

Anyway, as always, I would like to begin by thanking my Lord and Savior, through whom all things are possible, and to whom I am constantly praying, not only for the skill and courage to continue, but for light and peace and love, not only for myself and my loved ones, but for the world.

Thank you to my beautiful and supportive parents. They're such wonderful people, so funny and loving and brilliant. And yet they raised an author and a singer. I don't know where they went wrong.

Thank you to that singer, my twin soul and my best friend in the world, my sister KJ. I chose December 8th as this book's release date because it is the day after your birthday. My life infinitely changed for the better the night you were born. There's no one I would laugh with, watch scary movies with, shop with, or rock out to our favorite boy band with.

Thank you to my wonderful editors, Nancy, Kathleen, and Hannah. I'll admit, this release date kind of snuck up on us, and for that, I apologize! You are all so brilliant and wonderful and as soon as I get rich, I'm buying you all a car.

Actually, no, I probably will never be that rich. But I'll think of something.

Thank you to all my friends, Jessica, Rat, Rachel, Roxanne, Kat, Ali, Terri... I love you all more than words can say and I will always be thankful that you are in my life.

Thank you to all the amazing book bloggers and reviewers out there: April, Cassandra, Kendal, Lindsey, and so many others... I am so glad to have met all of you and to have connected with you over our shared love of reading and writing and books! Thank you for your wonderful words and for supporting authors the way that you do. You are so appreciated!

Thank you to the amazing librarians and library directors, who work tirelessly for readers of all ages, and who are gracious enough to host events for authors and readers to meet. I love you all so, so much.

Thank you to my fellow author friends. I'm sorry, there are far too many of you to list. But I love you all. Thank you for your books. Thank you for your friendship and your support. A special thank you to James and Claudette Peercy, for taking me under your wing and introducing me to a world full of new adventures. I am proud to be your duckling.

Finally, thank you, thank you, thank you to the readers. Without you, none of this would be possible. I wrote BOY BAND on a total whim (shout out to Savannah for talking me into trying NaNoWriMo!). I never dreamed it would lead to all this. Thank you. I love you. I love you. I love you.

JACQUELINE E. SMITH is the author of the CEMETERY TOURS series and the BOY BAND series. She is also featured in the horror anthology, LURKING IN THE DEEP. A longtime lover of words, stories, and characters, Jacqueline earned her Master's Degree in Humanities from the University of Texas at Dallas in 2012. She lives and writes in Dallas, Texas.

Made in the USA
Charleston, SC
21 March 2016